She led him through the pantry into the laundry room, tossed the clothes in the dryer, and set it on auto, then went back to the kitchen and put two cups of water in the microwave. When she looked up, he was grinning at her. His slicked-down hair, beginning to fluff up as it dried, made him look like a little kid. "What's so funny?" she asked defensively.

"Do you always bake your water?"

"It's a lot faster this way. See? It's already hot."

"Hey, okay," he laughed. "I'm all in favor of progress."

Laurie found some cookies in a cabinet, spread them on a plate, and carried it into the media room.

He came close and took a cookie from a plate she was holding. Her pulse beat a little faster. "Is that all you want?" she asked, teasing him.

He smiled crookedly, deepening the dimple in his chin. "For now," he said.

**Books
in the Couples series:**

COUPLES

SWORN ENEMIES

M.E. Cooper

BANTAM BOOKS

TORONTO • NEW YORK • LONDON • SYDNEY • AUCKLAND

SWORN ENEMIES

A Bantam Book

Produced by Cloverdale Press, Inc.,
133 Fifth Avenue, New York, NY 10003

ISBN 0 553 17270 0

Made and printed in Great Britain by
Hunt Barnard Printing Ltd., Aylesbury, Bucks.

SWORN ENEMIES

Chapter
1

Laurie Bennington sat down at one end of the long picnic table and watched Lars Olsen make his way to the counter to place their orders. Lars was nearing the end of his year as an exchange student at Kennedy High School, and he seemed determined to store up what he called "typical American experiences" to take back to Sweden with him. Their visit to the sub shop was a good example. Laurie would much rather have gone somewhere quieter and more intimate this afternoon. But to Lars, the sub shop was *the* place all the students went after school, going there was a "typical" thing to do.

Lars's broad shoulders and thatch of dark blond hair stood out in the crowd of kids at the counter. He turned for a moment and met Laurie's glance. His blue eyes, overshadowed by a craggy brow, seemed to bore into her. She imagined him schussing down an Alpine mountainside, expertly weav-

1

ing around flags, and easily cresting jumps that had sent other skiers tumbling. As he crossed the finish line in record time, his face, made ruddy by the winter sun, and the snowflake pattern of his heavy sweater were almost a blur, but he was not moving too fast to single Laurie out for a broad smile. She took a deep breath that turned into a sigh, and turned her head away.

A mirror on the wall returned Laurie's reflecttion. She studied it with a more critical eye than usual. Since meeting Lars, she had been letting her dark hair grow out, but it was still too short for real braids. Becoming a blonde was out of the question — she simply didn't have the nerve. And her father would go through the roof.

Then there was her dress. She had spent a long time looking through the shops before picking it out, but she still wasn't sure about it. The dark, print skirt, smocked bodice, and sheer white long sleeves were peasanty, all right, but were they *Swedish* peasanty? She had a horrible suspicion that she looked like someone from the cast of *The Sound of Music*. She wasn't sure where that had taken place — Switzerland or Austria, maybe — but she knew that it hadn't been Sweden.

At any rate, peasant girls didn't do a very good job of showing off their figures. Laurie knew perfectly well that she had a terrific body, and she liked to make sure that other people knew it, too. But in this flouncy skirt and smocked blouse, she could just as easily have had no figure at all. She knew her super outfits had helped make her the talk of Kennedy High, but she liked wearing the sort of clothes Lars was used to. It made her feel closer to him. And this dress was certainly a huge improvement over the bulky ski sweaters she had worn most of the winter. Her neck still itched when she thought of those sweaters.

She looked up. Lars was standing on the other side of the table studying her. She felt her cheeks grow warm. She was used to having guys look at her, but there was something in Lars's gaze that made her feel almost shy. Even though the table separated them, Laurie could almost feel heat coming from his eyes.

Behind the intense look, Lars seemed always to be lost in deep and serious thoughts. Finally, he spoke. "I was not sure if you wanted oil and vinegar or mayonnaise on your submarine. I thought mayonnaise. Is that all right?"

"Sure," she said, "that's fine."

"I am going to miss submarines," he continued, as he sat down. "In Sweden the only submarines we have belong to the navy." As usual, when he made a joke his face looked completely serious. It had taken Laurie weeks to learn when to laugh at one of them. Even now she sometimes laughed at his serious remarks, and nodded thoughtfully after a wisecrack.

"I hope that isn't all you're going to miss," she said, with a flirtatious look.

"Oh, no. I will miss many things: the shopping malls, and the expressways, and of course, the music videos. In my country we are still listening to the radio, even at home."

"Nothing else?" Laurie pouted.

Lars gave her an intense look that made her heart turn over. "One thing I will miss more than all the rest," he said. "One memory I will take back, to console me when I am lonely. I will remember the times we have spent together. And I will think that was America, that is what I have lost. I will be very sad, I think."

Laurie took a deep breath. "That's what I wanted to tell you," she said. "I've got some wonderful news. I had a chance to talk to my father last night. I had to do just about everything but stand on my head, but I finally got him to agree."

"Agree?" Lars said blankly. "Agree to what?"

"Why, to let me go with you. This summer," she added impatiently when he didn't respond. "To Sweden. Isn't that great?"

"You asked your father to let you come to Sweden?"

"That's right, and he said yes! But I've saved the best part for last. Listen to this. You know Daddy owns a cable TV station in Washington, D.C.?"

Lars nodded.

"Well, he said he's been thinking about featuring shows from countries other than the U.S. A lot of people in Washington come from other countries. He could do a French week, and an Italian week, maybe even a Chinese week, if they have much TV over there. The publicity would be super. Anyway, when I told him I wanted to spend the summer in Europe, he said that he can put me on the station's payroll as a special consultant. He'll put you on, too."

"Consultant?" Lars asked in a puzzled voice. "About what am I to consult? I am not an expert on anything."

4

"On television shows, of course! You know, the tastes of the younger generation, things like that. We can go all over, anywhere we want. And wherever we go, we'll get to meet all the important people in TV — actors, directors, celebrities, everybody. And the station will pay all our expenses. Isn't that fantastic?"

He shook his head slowly. "I don't think it would be correct for me to do this, Laurie. To go to serious people, artists, pretending to be what I am not. They would find out, and they would not approve."

"So what? Who cares what they think? Besides, you wouldn't be pretending. Daddy really does want to know what people our age think. We could help decide which shows are brought and shown here. No one's going to worry about whether we're experts or not if we can help them make a lot of money."

"Laurie, you do not understand," he said earnestly. "My country is not like the U.S.A. In the business community, everyone knows everyone, and everyone talks about everyone. It is very important to earn and keep the good opinion of people. If I did what you say, everyone would think that Lars has come back from America with a very swollen face."

"A *what*? Oh, you mean a swelled head."

"As you say. And twenty years from now, when I am asking for a new job or being thought of to be promoted, someone might say, Is he the one who went to America and came back pretending to be a big shot? So it is best that I act only as I truly am. Do you see?"

"No, I don't," Laurie replied, in an irritated voice. "But if you don't want to take Daddy up on his offer, I guess that's your right. I thought we could have a great time, that's all. And *I* can still go as a consultant and get my expenses paid. Don't worry, I won't tell anyone I know you."

The change in his expression made her instantly regret her spiteful words. "I'm sorry," she added, "I won't mention it again. Let's just think about all the fun things we can do together."

Instead of replying he picked up his sandwich in both hands and took an enormous bite, then stared down at his plate while he chewed. For a moment Laurie felt a chill between her shoulder blades, but she shrugged it off. She had learned that his actions didn't necessarily mean the same as those of an American boy.

Still not looking at her, he took a sip of his Pepsi, then cleared his throat. "My parents will already have plans for the summer, I think. It is a very funny time in Sweden, because it is so short and the winter is so long. Everyone becomes a little crazy with the sun. As a celebration of the summer solstice, on what you call Midsummer Eve, old friends get together and stay up all day and all night."

"It sounds fabulous! I can hardly wait!"

"Well, it is a very *Swedish* holiday. An American might think it is all very silly."

The chill returned to Laurie's spine. "Oh, Lars," she said, with a high-pitched laugh, "anybody listening to you would think that you don't *want* me to visit you this summer!" Then she paused expectantly, waiting for his denial and fervent invitation.

The silence stretched out, until she felt a scream of frustration gathering at the base of her throat. He wasn't going to protest her accusation.

"I do not want to leave you, Laurie. I will miss you very much. But it is important to know what is possible and what is not."

"Anything is possible if you're in love," she declared.

"I do not have the words I need to say this. For me you are my wonderful American girl who I will always remember. But soon I am leaving America and returning to my home in Sweden."

"Oh," Laurie said bitterly, "then I guess you'll have to find yourself a wonderful Swedish girl, right? Is that what you're trying to tell me?"

Two spots of bright red blossomed on his pale cheeks. "No, no. I am trying to tell you that I am going back to someone already."

"An ex-girl friend, you mean? Like a game of musical chairs?" Laurie knew her hurt and anger were taking over her tongue, and that at any moment she was going to say something she might regret for a long time. But she no longer cared about saying only what she knew would please Lars.

"Musical chairs? I do not know what is that. And no, Signe is not my ex-girl friend. We have been very, very close for years and years — since we were children. We cried heavy tears before I left to come here, and we have written many letters to each other."

7

"Really? How sweet. I'll bet you didn't write her about *me*."

"Of course I did. She asked to know all about you. Before I left, she told me that I would find a nice American girl to make my year less lonely. But I didn't believe her, I didn't think I could care for anyone, except Signe. But then I met you, and I discovered that she was correct after all. She was very happy to learn that."

A swirl of emotions surrounded Laurie. There was shame that the boy she had felt so close to was only on loan to her, and anger that he had waited until now to tell her this all-important fact about himself. But overshadowing both shame and anger was a sense of bewilderment like a dense gray fog, and a sort of unfamiliar fear.

She thought she knew Lars better than anyone in her life. She had wrapped herself in that knowledge as if in a warm, fluffy blanket. But now, suddenly, the blanket had been ripped away. She had to admit she didn't understand Lars at all, and obviously never had. She had fallen for someone she never knew.

Laurie didn't understand what he was saying about Signe either. No one who cared deeply for him would tell him to go find someone else, even if she knew that it was only for a little while. She was astonished and embarrassed to think that Lars actually mentioned her in his letters to Signe. She felt as if she had just been told of an unseen third at every movie, every drive through the country, and every evening she and Lars had spent in front of the TV. Laurie's face grew warm at the thought.

Now that Laurie thought back on it, Lars had never shown her any real signs of love. He was always polite and kind — even affectionate — but he never said anything to make her feel he was truly in love with her. What Laurie had taken for shyness, or his quiet Swedish style, was really Lars's way of staying distant, so he could go back to his childhood sweetheart. Laurie's face grew hot as she remembered the evenings they had spent together, evenings when she had shared her most secret dreams with Lars. Then she realized Lars had never really been hers; she had thrown her dreams away without a second thought.

Tears stung Laurie's eyes. She blinked them back. She was *not* going to start crying in the middle of the sub shop, not with half of Kennedy High sitting at the tables around her. Some of them would be only too pleased to see her upset, but she wasn't going to oblige them.

"This has made you sad," Lars said softly. "I'm sorry." He reached across the table to take her hand, but she jerked back.

"Sad? Me? No way!" She tried to give a laugh of derision, but it came out more like a groan. "I was just thinking what peculiar customs you people have. I suppose while you've been over here amusing yourself with me, Signe has been back home having a good time with a few other guys?"

The dull red spread from his cheeks to his forehead. "I have not been amusing myself with you, Laurie. I have cared very much. And you do not understand if you think that Signe would become attached to someone else. She is still in

Sweden, after all, among people who have known both of us all our lives. It is not the same."

Laurie snorted. "That's what she's letting you think. I'll bet her letters say she stays home watching television every night. Sure she does! And once you're back, no one will want to break the truth to you, will they?"

His eyes narrowed and the veins in his forehead stood out. "You are speaking very meanly," he said in a tight voice. "It is very unnecessary. You are not really a nasty person, I know. But sometimes you feel you have to act nasty. I have said I am sorry to upset you, and how much I have cared for you. But I do not care for you when you try to insult somebody you do not even know, only because you know I care for her, too. It is very low."

"Low? Well, what do you call what you did? We've been steadies since January! Don't you think that you could have told me that you were still in love with a girl back home? Did you have to let me make a fool of myself in front of the whole school, wearing those tacky, itchy sweaters and these cutesy-poo peasant costumes?"

"Didn't you like the clothes you wore? I would not ask you to change simply to please me. And I didn't tell you about Signe because I thought it would make you sad, instead of happy that we have had this time to share together. You have always known I would leave in the summer." Lars sighed. "Now you are sad and angry. And when you think of me after I am gone, you will not remember the wonderful hours, only the angry and sad feelings. That makes me sorry, too."

10

Laurie pushed her uneaten sandwich away and stood up abruptly. She knew that if she listened to Lars any longer, she would burst into tears. "I'm going home," she said. "I have to find Daddy and tell him that my summer plans have changed. Do you want me to drop you, or can you get a lift from one of the other kids?"

He looked at her steadily with those piercing blue eyes until she was forced to look away. "I think I walk back this afternoon," he said softly. "I have many things to think about."

"Suit yourself. Oh, and maybe you can find another ride to school tomorrow. I'm afraid it's not really convenient for me to pick you up." She didn't wait for his reply.

Chapter 2

"**P**heeb-a-rebop!" Woody Webster exclaimed. He slid down the bench next to Chris Austin and moved his tray out of the way. "You're just the one we need to talk some sense into these people."

Phoebe Hall smiled and took her place at the long table. She hadn't realized how much she enjoyed these afternoons at the sub shop with the gang until her parents grounded her for one month. Now that she was back in circulation, it took something really important to keep her away from the place.

"Talk sense?" she teased. "What makes you think I'll agree with you?"

"Oh, you will," Woody replied. "If logic doesn't work, I'll try intimidation. And if that fails, I'll bribe you."

"Why don't we go straight to the bribe then? Those look like good French fries." As she reached for one particularly crisp and inviting fry, he swatted her hand.

"Uh-uh-uh," he said. "Logic first, bribery later. I've been trying to get Chris to run for student government president. What do you think?"

"I think it's a super idea. Of course, she'll win by a landslide. What's the problem?"

"She says she won't run," Woody said.

"Oh? Why not?"

"I want Ted to run," Chris explained. Ted Mason was Kennedy's star quarterback and Chris's longtime boyfriend. "He'd make a better candidate, and a president than I would."

"But I said no," Ted said from the far end of the table. "I don't think I'd enjoy student politics very much."

"That's not the point," Chris replied. Her tone suggested she had explained the point more than once already. "You don't go into student government to have fun. It's an obligation. Kennedy High depends on the people who have talent and skills to carry their share of the load. If those people won't run, we'll end up with a bunch of officers who don't deserve our trust. I'm right, aren't I, Phoebe?"

"Well. . . ." Phoebe didn't exactly disagree with Chris, but she hadn't spent a lot of time contemplating the student government elections.

Woody took advantage of Phoebe's hesitation to jump in. "You're one thousand percent correct, Chrissie my girl. If people like you don't accept their obligations and take office, we'll end up with nothing but yo-yos and turkeys running things."

He was about to continue, but his girl friend Kim put her hand on his arm. "Chris," she said in a soft voice, "why do you think Ted would be better for the job? You've run the Honor Society for a year. You know how to manage an organization. Ted hasn't had that kind of experience, has he?"

"Nope," Ted replied. "What's more, I'm allergic to paperwork. Filling out any kind of form makes me break out in hives."

"And you've had experience as a candidate, too, Chris," Kim continued. "Not only that, you won."

Chris shifted uncomfortably on the bench. "That was different," she said. "I was running for homecoming princess, not student body president. Besides, I didn't really campaign. It was you guys who won the election, not me."

"And we'll win this one for you, too," Woody said. "Austin all the way! Yayyy!" He started clapping in an imitation of Kermit the Frog.

"Hold on, Woody," said Kim. She turned back to Chris. "I still don't understand. Why were you willing to run for homecoming princess but not for president?"

Phoebe thought she saw where Kim's questions were leading, and smiled to herself.

"Well, one was just an honorary post, and the other is for real."

"Don't you think you have the ability to be president?"

"Not as much as Ted, no. He's better qualified."

"Why?" Kim demanded, then turned to grin at Ted. "No offense."

"Well. . . ." Chris seemed at a loss for words.

"Do you think a woman could be qualified to be President of the United States?"

"Of course I do!"

"Then how about Kennedy High School, Rose Hill, Maryland?"

Instead of replying, Chris just pressed her lips together and shook her head.

Phoebe decided it was time to interfere. She knew, much better than Kim could, how Chris would react to being backed into a corner. At any moment she would refuse flatly to run or even to discuss it any longer. Once that happened, her pride would keep her from changing her mind.

"Chris," Phoebe said, "I need to get something from the drugstore. Will you please come with me?"

Kim glanced over quickly, as if she wanted to protest, but then she caught Phoebe's look and settled back.

"Sure," Chris replied. "I could use some fresh air. See you all later."

On the sidewalk, she turned to face Phoebe and said, "Thanks. By the time we get back, Woody will be on to some other crazy idea."

"What makes it so crazy?" Phoebe asked.

"Oh, come on! President of the student body? Me? The idea is ridiculous."

"I don't think so. But never mind that. Somebody's going to be president. Have you got a better candidate than yourself?"

15

"Of course I do: Ted."

"Who doesn't think he's qualified for the job, and doesn't want it anyway," Phoebe observed mildly.

"That's just modesty," Chris insisted, but she didn't sound very convincing.

"Is it? Look at Brad; he's been pretty good as president, hasn't he?" Brad Davidson, Phoebe's former boyfriend, was the outgoing student government head.

"Sure," Chris agreed. "He's been a lot better than 'pretty good.' "

"Why? Because he's conscientious, dedicated, hard-working, and fair, right? Now who does that describe better: you or Ted?"

Chris smiled reluctantly. Ted was thoroughly charming, with a smile that won over everyone and a genuine interest in others. He was as good a friend as anyone could hope to have. But no one would accuse him of being conscientious or hard-working. Even his considerable skill on the playing field came to him naturally, without any great effort.

"*Now* what do you say?" Phoebe said.

Chris turned halfway and looked out over the parking lot. "I didn't say Ted would be the same kind of president as Brad," she mumbled. "Of course he wouldn't. But in his own way he'd be just as good."

Phoebe grabbed Chris's shoulder and pulled her around. "Christine Alice Austin, you listen to me! You don't really believe what you're saying. What is going on here?" Chris's eyes shifted from side to side, as if she were looking for an escape path. Phoebe gave her a little shake. "Come on, Chris," she continued, "it's me, Phoebe. I'm your friend, remember? Talk to me!"

Chris said something in a voice too low for Phoebe to understand.

"What? I couldn't hear you."

"It's too silly," Chris repeated. "I'm ashamed to say it." She stopped and took a deep breath. "If I become president, I might lose Ted. And he matters more to me than anything! There! Now you can remind me of all the things I've ever said about civic duty and call me a real hypocrite."

Phoebe slipped an arm around her friend's shoulders. "Who, me? I'm no expert on civic duty. But I do think I know something about Ted Mason, and I can't imagine him giving you up even if you became the first woman to go to the moon."

"You don't know," Chris insisted. "He gets a lot of kidding already from other guys on the team. You know, jokes about being henpecked, stuff like that. It doesn't help that I'm president of the Honor Society. It got better after I became homecoming princess, because that's the kind of girl a football star is supposed to be going with, but now it's started up again. Think what they'll say if I become student body president! I don't even think there's ever been a girl in that office before."

"Not that I ever heard of," Phoebe said. "But who are these guys you're talking about? Everybody on the team likes Ted."

"Well . . . the worst one is John Marquette."

"John Marquette!" Phoebe exclaimed. Marquette was a champion wrestler as well as defensive guard on the football team. He was also, in his own mind, the most irresistible male at Kennedy High. "Look, Chris, Marquette tries to tear down anybody other people respect. He used to hassle Brad so much that Brad almost punched him in the locker room. The coach had to break it up. Can you imagine Brad punching anybody? That just shows you what Marquette is like."

"I *know* what he's like! That's why I don't want to expose Ted to that kind of treatment."

"You can't protect him from it, even now. And if he becomes president, there'll be plenty of jealous types like Marquette giving him a hard time every day, whatever either of you do."

"But if *I* become president, Ted might feel — oh, I don't know, neglected or something — coming second. He might decide that he'd rather hang out with some gushy sophomore, who can't talk about anything except what a big football hero he is. Things like that do happen, you know."

"Not to people like Ted," Phoebe said grimly. "And if he did pull a low stunt like that, it would prove that he's not the guy you thought he was. Chris, he's *proud* of you! He's not trying to compete with you. He doesn't need to. He's happy being who he is, and he's happy with you being who you are."

Chris's eyes glistened. "Do you really think so? Because if I did something that made me lose him, I'd never forgive myself."

Phoebe squeezed her shoulders. "I'm *sure* of it. Now let's go back in there and start planning your campaign to become the first female president of Kennedy High!"

Chris thought about Phoebe's arguments as she and Ted strolled on the lawn of Rosemont Park, a pre-Revolutionary estate that had been given to the town by the last of its founding families. As usual, no one else was there. Most people preferred Rose Hill Park, on the other side of town, which had tennis courts, a swimming pool, and even an outdoor theater. Rosemont had nothing, except a series of old formal gardens gradually returning to their natural state.

They wandered hand in hand along a path through the trees that came out at the edge of a low bluff. Chris sank down onto the grass and pulled Ted down next to her. By a trick of the terrain this spot had a view of rolling meadows and woods that seemed to go on forever, though in fact, the nearest house was within shouting distance. To their left, the sky was still a pure, pale blue. In the other direction the setting sun was tinting the few high clouds in faint shades of pink and purple. The evening breeze found its way through the opening of Chris's jacket and made her shiver. Ted put his arm around her, and she snuggled back into the welcome warmth.

"Don't you wish we could stay here like this forever?" she sighed.

"Um-hum. But it'll be suppertime before long. Do you think we could arrange for meals to be sent in?"

"You!" She turned her head and tried to nip his hand, but he evaded her teeth and lightly tweaked her nose. "Ouch," she exclaimed. "Ted Mason, you're about as romantic as a trip to traffic court!"

"Gee, I thought you just wanted to keep warm and admire the view."

"Oh! You're infuriating!" She started to pummel his ribs, but he clasped his arms around her. When she tried to protest, he silenced her with his lips. As always, an electric current surged between them, robbing her of her breath, leaving her unaware of anything but the closeness of him.

Finally, Ted's arms relaxed and Chris pulled back, propping herself on her elbows. His wavy blond hair was full of pine needles. She started pulling them out one by one, chanting: "He loves me, he loves me not, he loves me. . . ."

He grinned. "If it doesn't come out right, I'll stick in a few more for you. Some went down the neck of my shirt, too. Do they count?"

"I don't know." Her expression became grave. "Ted? Are you really glad? About my running? You weren't just saying that because of the others, were you?"

"Hey, I'm planning to get hired as your secretary. Anyone who wants to talk to the Prez has to pay me off first. If I work this right, it could finance my way through college!"

"Please, Ted, I mean it. If I thought for one minute that this was going to come between us, I'd go right back and tell everyone to find another candidate."

He sat up and put his hands on her shoulders. "Okay, seriously then. I think you'll make a terrific president. And I know I'll be proud to sit in the middle of an otherwise dismal school assembly and say, That's my girl."

"And if you ever start to feel different, do you promise to tell me?"

"I do. But I want a promise from you, too, that you'll never ask me to go anywhere with you that I'll have to wear a tie."

"You doofus!" She grabbed a handful of pine needles and scattered them over his head. "What about the Senior Prom?"

"That's different; I ask you. I'm very old-fashioned about some things."

Chapter
3

The rains earlier in the week had brought the Potomac River to its spring crest. It thundered over and around the rocks, boiling up in sheets of white foam that floated downstream on the surface of the brown water. The breeze carried a fine mist of spray all the way up to the over-look where Laurie stood. She rubbed her moist cheeks, and wiped away the mingled spray and tears.

She had not meant to come here. It almost seemed as if her little Mustang had found its own way. Great Falls Park had been a favorite place of hers, ever since she stumbled across it one day a few weeks after moving to Rose Hill. It was close enough to come to often, but far enough to be an escape. She had never seen anyone she knew here. If she ever did, it might ruin the place for her.

Once, a few weeks earlier, she had brought

Lars to Great Falls. It hadn't been easy to do; she felt as though she was showing him a very private part of herself, a part she never revealed to the kids at Kennedy. She still wasn't sure what she had hoped the visit would do; but whatever it was, it hadn't happened. In fact, the trip was a big disappointment.

When she brought Lars up to this overlook he had dutifully admired the view of the falls, then studied the brochure he had picked up at the park entrance to find out what the total vertical drop was. He also informed her that the overgrown ruins across the way were the remains of a mill and foundry once owned by the Custis family. She hadn't known that, and she wasn't at all sure that she wanted to. For some reason she preferred simply to think of them as ruins. As they started back to Rose Hill, he thanked her for a very educational excursion.

Laurie leaned on the log railing and stared down at the racing water far below. She should have realized Lars was not the boy she wanted him to be — that afternoon should have warned her. She had wanted so badly for it to work. But each time something like that happened, she told herself he was a foreigner, that the things he did and said didn't necessarily mean what they seemed to. She kept hoping he would change; it was a mistake she would not make again.

Laurie glanced over at the sign warning park visitors not to climb on the rocks that banked the river. The thought of falling and crashing into rocks and being pulled underwater unnerved her momentarily, but she found a certain satisfaction in imagining what would happen afterward. When the news of her death reached Lars, he would regret the way he had treated her and realize, too late, that she was his one true love. All her classmates would attend the funeral, marvel at her sacrifice, and tell each other how sorry they were that they hadn't gotten to know her better. The park authorities might even change the name of this spot to Lovers Leap, and those who really knew the story would call it Laurie's Leap instead.

The muddy foam was churning downstream, creating small whirlpools among the immense gray rocks that jutted from the water. Laurie gazed into the center of one of the swirling eddies until she felt herself grow dizzy.

She closed her eyes and grabbed the railing. After a moment the dizziness passed, and she swallowed, took a deep breath, and shook her head. She laughed at her own theatrics. Had she actually thought of throwing herself into a filthy river over a *boy*? The world was full of boys much sexier and better-looking than Lars, who would flip over her as soon as they met her. She simply hadn't made enough of an effort to find them yet, but that was going to change.

Laurie turned and walked over to the parking lot. Before driving off, she put down the top and tied her hair back with a scarf. She knew she drew people's glances in her red convertible, and that was just what she wanted. With any luck, she would meet the boy of her dreams before Lars returned to Sweden. She imagined herself walking arm in arm with her dream boy past the lonely and jealous Swede, not even sparing him a glance. Without even looking she would know that the look on Lars's face betrayed his knowledge that he had carelessly thrown away a real treasure.

It was almost dark by the time Laurie pulled into her driveway and stopped in front of the garage. Her father's car wasn't there — that was a relief. She was not looking forward to telling him that the scheme they had agreed on only the day before had just gone down the tubes. Of course, she could simply not tell him. If she didn't say anything more about the summer, the plan might slip his mind.

Laurie wrapped her arms around herself and shivered. Spring or not, it wasn't really top-down weather yet. She flicked the switch that controlled the power top, but nothing happened. She pressed it harder. After a long moment, she heard the familiar whine of the electric motor, and from behind her the dark canvas rose up to block out the evening sky. A flip of the latches fastened it to the windshield, buttoning up the Mustang for the night.

Mrs. Byrne, the housekeeper, had left a casserole in the oven, and salad and pie in the refrigerator. Laurie dropped her books on the kitchen table, fixed herself a plate of food, and poured a glass of soda, then carried her dinner into the media room. Unlike the formal and cold living room, this room was used every day. It stretched across the back of the house, with big windows that overlooked the yard and the pool. However, few people who entered the room bothered to look out the windows. They were too fascinated by the huge, retractable screen of the projection TV, the cabinets of state-of-the-art stereo and video equipment, and the antique Wurlitzer jukebox whose multicolored neon tubes bubbled endlessly when it was switched on.

Laurie was so used to all the gadgetry, she hardly noticed it. She slumped down onto the couch, picked up the remote control, and pushed a few buttons. The screen descended from its hiding place in the ceiling and burst into color. The regular channels were all broadcasting news or showing reruns of ancient sitcoms. She tried the music channel and found a Madonna video she had seen a hundred times before. She pushed the scan button and watched the pictures flit past: a weather map, news headlines, a drama in Spanish, five people talking around a coffee table, a diagram of the digestive system, and two different dumb cartoons. Boring, boring, *boring!*

With an exasperated sound she zapped the TV, tossed the remote control on the couch, and began to prowl around the room. The two shelves of videocassettes and four shelves of records didn't merit even a glance. Once she had shown them proudly to Lars and drunk in his amazement, but tonight they seemed meaningless. If they couldn't take her mind off the pain of Lars's betrayal, what use were they?

For the hundredth time, Laurie contemplated what she might do to win Lars back, and she played over her memory of the afternoon. Was there any point at which she could have made it all right by saying something different? Had she

26

driven him away by her anger and possessiveness? But the more she thought about it, the more clearly she realized the truth: Lars had always been on loan to her, and the term of the loan had just run out. She had never really had a chance with him. All her peasant dresses, and knickers, and reindeer-covered sweaters did not make her a bit more Swedish; if anything, they made her look ridiculous.

Laurie's face flushed as she recalled once again his bland statement that he had told Signe about her and gotten her approval. How she would love to see what he had said about her in his letters! Had he made their relationship sound less important than it was, to keep his Swedish girl friend from getting worried? Or had he made it sound *more* important, to get her jealous?

Laurie realized she would never know the truth. She would never know how much she had meant to him. As if the obstacles of different languages and cultures were not enough to keep her in the dark, there was his deliberate deception. How often he had told her stories about his life in Sweden, without ever breathing a word about Signe! All the times he talked about his "friend" and he doing something — overturning a canoe on a freezing lake and drying off around a fire afterwards, hitchhiking across the country to sneak into an Abba concert, or going on three-day-long cross-country ski tours — he had probably meant Signe. He hadn't ever mentioned the friend's name.

The more Laurie thought about it, the more she felt Lars had used her. She had never been anything more to him than a summer romance that happened to take place in winter — a way to keep himself entertained during his stay in a strange country, a free guide to American customs and culture. The clearer the situation became, the more Laurie's pain and sadness turned into anger. She had been treated badly, and she deserved the satisfaction of getting back at the person who had mistreated her. Lars had to find out that he couldn't do that to an American girl and get away with it.

But Laurie couldn't tell people how Lars tricked her without making herself look like a fool, and that was the last thing she wanted. Besides, what she really needed was to take her mind off his deception, not to dwell on it constantly.

She could make him jealous. She could start being seen with some gorgeous hunk right away. There was John Marquette, for instance; he had shown an interest in her often enough. Not that John was very exclusive in his interests; he also had pursued that strange Sasha Jenkins. Still, he *was* interested, and he had all the muscles any guy could want. Too bad he had muscles between his ears, too. She imagined spending an evening listening to him describe his latest wrestling match, and decided that there had to be some better way of getting revenge.

She paused in her prowling to look out the window. The water in the pool reflected a light from the house next door. The weather would be warm enough for swimming in another week or two. She could throw a fantastic party, one that would be the talk of the whole school, and not invite Lars.

The party Laurie had thrown the year before, right after moving to Rose Hill, had instantly made her an important person at Kennedy High. Her second attempt, in the fall, hadn't been that big a success. Chris Austin had shown her true character by getting drunk halfway through the evening, supposedly after breaking up with her boyfriend. When her friends decided to take her home, it broke things up early.

Laurie decided it ought to be a swimming party, starting late on a Saturday afternoon, going on through dinner and into the night. That would give people plenty of time to get really loose. She would have to get a caterer to supply the food. Kim Barrie's mother catered for lots of important Washington people; maybe she would do it. And she could ask Peter Lacey to turn her on to some hot new local band that was still small enough to play at parties. Her dad wouldn't mind picking up the bills, as long as she made it clear that her friends had important parents, and she didn't expect him to make an appearance. That was fine with her; she rated parents at parties about equal to ants at picnics.

Lars would hear all about the party the following Monday morning, of course. And even as he was pounding the wall over missing the biggest social event of the semester, he would also have to think up a way to explain why *he* hadn't been there. He might say that he had had a toothache, or he had been out of town, or that parties were against his principles. Or he might tell the truth, that he hadn't been invited.

Laurie frowned at her reflection in the window-pane. If Lars *did* tell the truth, it might make her look like the bad guy, and win him sympathy he didn't deserve. In fact, he wouldn't be the only one to face awkward questions. Everyone knew she was seeing Lars seriously. Her guests would ask where he was. There was no way she could tell people what happened between her and Lars without looking ridiculous, and not inviting him would seem so petty. Some people might even guess that her real motive for giving the party was to leave him off the guest list. That would make for the wrong talk on Monday morning. Suddenly, the party didn't seem like such a good idea.

Whatever she did, it had to be more subtle than a blatant brush-off. It couldn't seem the least bit directed at Lars. Even *he* shouldn't know that it was aimed at him. She began to pace again. Halfway across the room, she noticed her dirty plate still sitting on the coffee table. She was tempted to leave it for Mrs. Byrne to clear away in the morning. Then she recalled the way her father had scolded her for not cleaning up after herself. This was no time to get on his bad side. She picked up the plate and glass, rinsed them at the kitchen sink, and stuck them in the rack of the dishwasher.

The latest issue of *The Red and the Gold*, the Kennedy student newspaper, was on top of her pile of textbooks. She scanned the front page idly, then read with sharper interest. The lead story announced the upcoming student elections, and explained how to file a petition to become a candidate. According to the paper, the process had been changed a couple of years earlier. The result was that cliques could no longer play an important role in student government.

Laurie gave a lopsided grin. Maybe Sasha Jenkins, the editor of the paper, didn't recognize how much power certain cliques at Kennedy really held, but Laurie did. That was how, less than two months after transferring to the school, she had gotten appointed to the post of student activities officer. She wasn't likely to be reappointed next year, though, not after making an enemy of Chris Austin and her sleazoid stepsister Brenda. At least, not if that crowd continued to control student government.

But Laurie wasn't sure she wanted to be reappointed. Not if she was going to be upstaged by people like that peculiar Woody Webster, who organized the Follies and the fashion show, and somehow managed to be taken seriously despite his inclination to wear purple high-top sneakers. She could easily be an *elected* officer. She would certainly win if she ran — practically everyone in school knew her. She had a couple of important enemies, but their votes didn't count any more heavily than those of some freshman nobodies. And her victory would show Lars how popular she really was, yet no one would ever think to connect her running with their breakup.

Ideas began to tumble over one another. She would have posters printed with a sultry photo of her and some catchy slogan, and get them put up all over school and around town. And what about a sixty-second commercial, with musical background, to be played every lunch hour on Peter Lacey's show? Her father could probably get a few local celebrities to attend a rally in the quad a day or two before the voting. She might even decide to throw that swimming party after all, as a way of kicking off her campaign.

As Laurie envisioned her posters, she realized she'd have to choose an office to run for. Not class representative — too ordinary. And being president was too much work — Brad Davidson, the current president, was always busy with SG affairs. Treasurer was out, she hated arithmetic, and the title of secretary had too much of a horn-rimmed-glasses and pencil-behind-the-ear sound to it. By elimination then, Laurie Bennington would be the next vice-president of the Kennedy High School Student Government Association. And Lars Olsen could go back to his drab little Swedish girl knowing that he had thrown away his chance to be associated with someone of real stature.

Chapter 4

"Hey, Cardinals, this is when the day really starts! WKND is on the air again!"

Sasha Jenkins smiled as the lunchroom loudspeaker blared into life. Peter had so much fun doing his regular noontime rock show. And he made it so obvious he was having fun, that even those who didn't like his taste in music listened.

"Yes indeed," the voice continued in an imitation of a top-forties DJ. "This is Spacey Lacey spinning them at you as fast and hard as he can throw. Catch them if you dare. Firing up turntable number one, here's the very latest from The Boss himself, the pride of Asbury Park." The voice faded as the opening notes of a Bruce Springsteen hit sounded out.

"Hi, Sasha. Are you meditating?"

Sasha blinked and refocused her eyes. Phoebe had just sat down across the table from her. She

33

was wearing her favorite Cub Scout shirt, Sasha noticed. The boy who had originally owned it must have been really gung ho; there were half a dozen arrowheads under each of the three patches on the pocket.

Phoebe began a futile attempt to rip open the plastic covering of her tuna-salad sandwich. "Try your teeth," Sash advised. "You'll break a nail that way if you're not careful."

"Ha!" Phoebe said grimly. "I don't even like tuna that much, but a girl in my Bio. class told me it contains some mineral that strengthens your nails."

Sasha frowned in concentration. "I never heard that," she said, shaking her head. "Good nails need calcium, I know, but the best source of that is milk."

"Ha!" Phoebe repeated. "On Monday I tore a nail opening a carton of milk. It spilled all over my jeans, too. I had to go around that way for the rest of the day. It's enough to make me give up lunch altogether, which wouldn't be such a terrible idea," she added, patting her tummy.

Sasha smiled. Phoebe's figure was definitely on the curvy side, but no one would accuse her of having a weight problem. "You could bring your lunch from home," she observed, motioning toward her container of granola and yogurt, and her cheddar cheese sandwich on wheatberry bread. "It's healthier, and a lot cheaper, too."

Phoebe shook her red curls and laughed. "It's a battle just to get myself out of the house in the morning. Even if I remembered to make a lunch, I'd probably leave it in the fridge half the time."

Sasha reached across the table and touched her hand. "It's great to see you so cheerful again, Phoebe," she said.

"I had a bad winter," Phoebe admitted. "It was bad enough to have Griffin go off to New York like that, only a few days after we had fallen in love. But then when he told me not to call him anymore, and dropped out of sight completely, I didn't know what to think. I tried to imagine what terrible thing I had done to make him treat me that way."

"That's ridiculous! *You* hadn't done anything, it wasn't your fault."

"I know that now, but I didn't then. Besides, I don't think it's right to talk about fault. What he did hurt me a lot, but he didn't mean to hurt me. He was trying to protect me, in a way."

"Huh. Well, I forgive him if you do," Sasha said. "But I still don't think much of his explanation."

"Look at it from his point of view," Phoebe said earnestly. "After he told me about his wonderful success, getting a part in a Broadway play, and an apartment in Greenwich Village, it all vanished overnight. The part went to someone else, the agent who told him to come to New York dropped him, and the only place he could afford to live was a tiny apartment in a tenement somewhere that he shared with three other guys. He was too proud to let me see it all."

"As if you'd have cared. Didn't he trust you to go on loving him, even if he wasn't an instant star?"

"I know, I know," Phoebe sighed. "I told him

35

the same thing myself, but it's too much a part of him. It isn't that he didn't trust me, either. He just couldn't feel good about himself. He would have spent the whole time we were together expecting to see pity in my face, when he wanted to see pride instead. He couldn't have taken that."

"When are you two going to get together again? Three days wasn't much time, after you'd been apart for so long."

Phoebe traced a pattern on the tabletop with her fingertip. "I'm not sure. He's determined to get his diploma now, so he's studying very hard all the time. Between that and acting school, and whatever job he manages to get, he doesn't have much free time."

"Well, I don't care," Sasha said. "I think you ought to go up there and see him. If he has to work while you're there, you can go sit in the library or take a tour of the Empire State Building or something."

"*If* he invites me, and *if* I can get permission from my parents, I'd go in a second," Phoebe replied with a determined toss of her head.

Phoebe bent over her tray, pulling at the wrapping of her sandwich again. Suddenly she sat up and said, "*Argh!*" She glared down at the tiny tear in the plastic wrap and the larger tear in the nail of her left ring finger.

"What's the trouble?" a new voice asked. Brad was approaching the table, tray in hand. His faded polo shirt, neatly creased khakis, and well-polished loafers made him look exactly like the

36

sort of guy who would be going off to Princeton in September.

"Hi, Sash, Phoebe," Brenda said from behind him. "What's up?" She was in pegged black jeans and a white buttondown shirt the size of a small tent. Two geometric earrings in black and white plastic dangled from her right ear. She didn't look at all like the kind of girl who would be going with a guy who would be going to Princeton.

Sasha was one of the few people who had accepted the two as a couple from the beginning. By now, though, everybody had to admit that they had worked out really well. The security and acceptance Brad gave Brenda had helped her to take the chip off her shoulder. While her offbeat, irreverent attitudes were helping to make him a little less stiff and staid.

"I broke my nail," Phoebe explained gloomily. "That makes two this week."

"Who needs sharp nails anyway?" Brad asked, glancing down at his hands. "If you ask me, doctors have the right idea: Keep them super short and super clean."

"You're right, Brad," Phoebe said thoughtfully. "Maybe the fact that I can't grow nails should guide me toward a career in medicine."

Brad looked at her, his eyes wide with horror, but Sasha and Brenda giggled along with Phoebe.

The music in the background faded and Peter's voice boomed, "There you go, three in a row! After The Boss, we heard a cut by a new English group called the Sharks . . . something fishy there, if you ask me. And that was followed by an instrumental that's making a splash on the charts, by a group called Loud Voices. Hey listen, guys, I'm not making this up, you know!"

Everybody at the table smiled. Brad was about to say something when Peter continued, "A little news before we choose to abuse the grooves. As *ev*-erybody knows, we've got elections coming up real soon. If you're planning to run for office, you'd better get to work collecting signatures on your petition. They have to be turned in by Monday. Lots of rumors going 'round about who's running for what, but I said this was news, and rumors aren't news. This is, though: It's a classy cut by the Stones that was on the English version of the album, but not on the one they released here. Rock on, Cardinals!"

As Peter brought the driving beat up to cover his voice, Sasha said, "I bumped into Chris by the lockers before. She told me she's decided to run for president." Sasha had expected a big commotion. Instead, she was met with quiet nods of agreement. "You guys all know that already? Sometimes the press are the last people to find out what's going on."

"She only decided late yesterday," Phoebe said.

"She told me when she got home last night," Brenda said.

"And Brenda told me this morning," Brad added. "So you weren't so late in finding out, after all. Have you heard anything about the other candidates yet?"

"Not officially," Sasha admitted. "And as Peter just said: Rumors aren't news. I have a feeling that it isn't going to be a very crowded race, though. People don't seem as interested in running for office as they used to."

"It's a dog's life," Brad joked. "I have calluses on my fingers from signing all those official documents, and I'm nearly deaf from all the times I've had to listen to 'Hail to the Chief.'"

Sasha exchanged a glance with Phoebe. Two or three months before Brad would never have been able to poke fun at himself that way. Brenda had certainly succeeded in teaching him not to take himself so seriously.

"Clean cups! Clean cups! Move down!" Woody put his tray down next to Phoebe's, and made shooing motions at them with his hands.

Sasha smiled. No one had ever had to teach Woody not to take himself too seriously. He had been born with a light heart and a strong sense of the ridiculous, along with a tremendous fund of loyalty.

He reached over and touched Phoebe's red hair. "Well, Pheebarooni, are you starting to yearn for the spotlight again?" he said. As director of the Kennedy Follies the previous fall, Woody had been responsible for Phoebe's singing debut — a duet with Griffin that stole the show.

"You're dreaming up another of your projects," Phoebe accused.

"What if I am?" he retorted. "Didn't everyone love the follies? Wasn't the *Vogue/GQ* fashion show the talk of the school?"

"And didn't we have to work all day and night to pull it off?"

"No pain, no gain," he replied in a deep voice.

"Oh no," Brenda groaned, "Kim has talked him into staging a Kennedy High version of *Pumping Iron!*"

The others laughed. The most recent event at Kennedy had been the run-a-thon Kim organized to raise money for the girls' track team. Woody, who usually scorned anything in the way of organized sports, had almost run himself into a state of collapse in an attempt to impress her.

"Say, where *is* Kim?" Sasha asked. "I haven't seen her all day."

It was Woody's turn to groan. "As if she weren't busy enough already, helping her mom run the catering business — she's appointed herself Chris's campaign manager. The two of them are prowling around, grabbing freshmen, and twisting their arms to sign Chris's petition."

"Why freshmen?" Phoebe asked "Why don't they ask us? *I'd* sign."

Woody tapped his forehead. "Strategy, Pheeb-a-rebop, deep, deep strategy. It's all Kim's idea. Sure, Chris could fill up her petition with the names of people who are friends of hers, but why do that? We'll support her anyway. But if you get people you don't know to help, you make them feel involved. They'll not only vote for you, they'll try to get their friends to vote for you, too."

"Hmm," said Phoebe. "I'm impressed. It sounds as if she's planning to run a real campaign. But who is she going to be running against? I can't think of anybody in our class who would stand a chance against her. Look at the way she won the homecoming princess title last fall."

Brad looked solemn. "We'll know about that on Monday, when the petitions are filed. But I wouldn't take anything for granted. This is a pretty big school, you know."

Chapter
5

Laurie tucked the completed petition into her notebook, dropped the pen in her purse, and adjusted the wide neck of her royal-blue silk blouse to expose a shapely, well-tanned shoulder. "Thanks," she said to the guy from her English class who had provided the last signature. She glanced at her watch; she still had plenty of time for lunch.

"Uh, sure," he replied, backing away and keeping his eyes on her. "Good luck."

She had already forgotten that he existed. As she walked down the corridor toward the quad, she asked herself once again if she really wanted to run for office. She had not enjoyed going around with her petition. Asking people to sign it seemed too much like begging, and she hated to beg for anything. Whether the person you asked agreed or not, he ended up on top. If he said yes, you owed him a favor, and if he said no, he had proven that he was in a position to reject you.

That was why she had avoided taking the petition to anyone she knew at all well. Instead, she had landed on those who looked sort of familiar, or who seemed timid enough to sign without discussion. Her judgment wasn't perfect; one meek-looking sophomore had demanded to know where she stood on equal funding for student clubs.

The truth was she had never given it a moment's thought, but she couldn't admit that. She tried to say that the issue had many sides to it. The sophomore then gave her a lecture on why the Outing Club deserved more money per member than the Spanish Club. His argument was that it cost a lot to take students on rock-climbing and spelunking trips. Laurie was tempted to say that it would cost a lot to take them to Spain, too. When he finally walked off, without signing, Laurie resolved that once she was elected, she would do whatever she could to ruin the Outing Club.

As Laurie approached the quad, Lars walked by across the way. It was the first time she had seen him since leaving the sub shop the previous afternoon. She had been dreading this moment, and contemplated her options. She could start screaming insults at him, pretend not to know him, or nod coolly as she passed.

For a moment, she was flooded with a desire to run after him and throw her arms around him. He couldn't have really said good-bye like that; she had misunderstood him. If she just reminded him of how much they cared for each other, they could work out whatever the problems were.

The memory of every moment of closeness they had shared raced through her mind. She hadn't imagined them; they really had happened. She knew every detail so well. She had recalled them night after night as she was going to sleep. She couldn't give them up just like that, it would leave her with nothing.

Lars was out of sight. Tears welled up in her eyes. She silently begged for him to come back, to hold and kiss her, and assure her that it would all be all right. The knowledge that he wasn't going to, that he would never hold her again, made her want to sob aloud.

If she had been alone, she might have done it. But the thought of the spectacle she would make going to pieces in the middle of the quad, kept her on her feet. Angrily she wiped at her eyes with the back of her hand. Lars did not love her and never had. She had thrown herself into the relationship, but he had deliberately kept an important part of himself back. Even their closest moments had been a lie. He had held her, yes, but he was probably imagining Signe's face.

"Hi," someone called from behind her.

Laurie blinked a couple of times, to dry her eyes before looking around. A brown-haired girl in a Hawaiian-print shirt, denim mini-skirt, and pink plastic flats was walking across the grass toward her, smiling confidently. Her face and her asymmetrical haircut looked familiar, but Laurie couldn't think who she was or where they had met. "Hi," she replied.

"I'm Gloria Macmillan," the girl continued. "We met at the party after the *Vogue/GQ* show. You probably don't remember, but we talked a long time about the outfit you modeled. It just blew me away."

All Laurie could remember was being pestered with questions by some sophomore. "Of course, Gloria, how are you?"

"Fine. Listen, I was so excited to hear that you're running for vice-president. You're just exactly what this moldly place needs to put some life into it."

"Thanks," Laurie said, preening a little. "I didn't know the word had gotten around yet."

"Oh, when someone like you does something, people notice. A friend of mine told me he'd signed your petition, and I was just thrilled. I decided that I just *had* to help."

"Help? Well, thanks, Gloria, that's really sweet of you, but I already have all the signatures I need."

"That's terrific, but that isn't what I mean. I want to help in your campaign. You know, pass out leaflets, talk to people, put up posters, stuff like that. Who's going to be your campaign manager?"

"I haven't had time to give it much thought yet," Laurie admitted.

"Oh, you should, really. There's not much time before the election, is there?" Her smile became a little secretive. "And we don't want your opponent to get the jump on you."

"Opponent?" Laurie said sharply. "What opponent?"

"Didn't you know? My friend was asked to sign a petition for someone else who wants to run for vice-president, too. I guess he looks like the petition-signing sort," she added with a slight laugh.

Laurie tried to smile back, but her mind was racing. It hadn't really occurred to her that anyone would run against her. Somehow it didn't seem fair. "Who is it?" she asked. "What's her name?"

"Not her, him," Gloria replied. "His name's Richard Westergard."

Laurie thought for a moment, then shook her head. "Never heard of him. Is he a junior?"

"I guess so. My friend told me he's captain of the chess team and a big noise in the Computer Club. My friend's sort of into computers, too, that's how he knows him."

Laurie gave a short laugh and relaxed. For a moment she had been worried that she might be facing a dangerous opponent. No wonder she didn't know Westergard; he sounded like Supernerd. She could imagine him: very short, with big ears, curly hair, thick glasses, and a terrible complexion. He probably wore wrinkled gray pants, thin white socks, black lace-up shoes, and a striped long-sleeve shirt with half a dozen pens stuffed into one of those plastic pocket protectors.

"He doesn't sound like much of a threat," she remarked.

"Don't be too sure," Gloria said. "A lot of kids might vote for him because they figure that somebody with a scientific background will run things more efficiently."

"Efficiency isn't everything," Laurie said defensively.

"Oh, I *know*, I couldn't agree more. That's why I think it's so important for you to get elected, to give student government a sense of *style*. If there's anybody at Kennedy that has a real sense of style, it's you."

Laurie thought that was an exaggeration. She could think of several other girls she considered stylish. And of course, there was Henry Braverman, whom everyone was calling a brilliant designer. Still, it was nice to hear some flattery, especially when her self-esteem had just suffered such a blow from Lars. And she certainly had a better sense of style than some chess and computer freak!

"Well. . . ." she demurred.

"In fact," Gloria continued enthusiastically, "if I were running your campaign, I'd make that your slogan. 'Vote for Laurie Bennington — for a student government with STYLE!' "

Laurie adjusted the neckline of her blouse and tilted the wide belt around her hips to a more rakish angle. "You don't think that might sound a little, you know, superficial?"

"Of course not! This is the era of style, isn't it? Look at all the designers who appear on TV talk shows. Besides, having style doesn't mean you won't do anything important. It just means that when you do, you'll do it with a little flash, so everyone will sit up and take notice."

"That's important," Laurie said with a nod. "How many people pay attention to what student government is doing now?"

Gloria gave a snort of derision.

"Exactly," Laurie continued. "When I became student activities officer, I tried to make students more aware of what was going on, but I was tripped up everywhere I turned. The fact is, some of the people who are running things now don't really want the rest of us to know too much about what they're doing. That's one of the reasons I'm running for vice-president: to make student government more responsive, and more open."

"Fantastic! Wow, I wish I had my tape recorder with me, Laurie. That is *exactly* what all the kids I know are just waiting to hear. If we could only play that every day on KND, you'd win by a landslide!"

Laurie blinked. "Do you really think so?" she asked in surprise. Then she hastily added, "Naturally, I gave a lot of thought to these matters before I decided to run. It's only that I wasn't sure that the voters were ready for my message yet."

"Oh, of course they are — ready and waiting," Gloria said eagerly. "All you have to do is reach them. That's why I asked who is going to manage your campaign. You have to find somebody who really believes in you and what you stand for, and has the enthusiasm to get the word out."

Laurie smiled confidently, but inwardly she was frowning. Where was she going to find someone like that? She had easily filled her petition, true, but none of the signers had been terribly enthusiastic. She knew a lot of people, of course, but many of them were too close to Chris Austin to be willing to help her openly. The most she could expect from them was encouragement. She couldn't think of anyone who had both the personality and the enthusiasm to be an effective campaign manager.

Why hadn't she given more thought to what running for office involved? She had gone into it on the assumption that she would file her petition and everybody would say, "Laurie, of course," then she would be the next vice-president. It still might turn out that way, but the presence of a new competitor, even one as ignorable as what's-his-name, made a big change in the situation. If she simply coasted along, assuming that she was going to win, she might allow Captain Chess to beat her. Instead of a triumph her run for office would turn into a humiliation as painful as her breakup with Lars — even more painful, perhaps, because everybody at Kennedy High would be aware of it.

No question about it, she had to mount a serious campaign. The first, essential step was to find a serious campaign manager, which brought her back to her starting point: She didn't know where she was going to find one.

Gloria didn't seem to have noticed her thoughtfulness. "Wow," she said, "I am really, *really* excited about your running. Ever since I heard, I keep having more ideas about how to get your message across. Like, what if you got someone to come up with a really nifty design to put on a T-shirt? You know how everybody flips over unusual T-shirts. You could probably raise money for the campaign selling them. And whenever anybody wore one, she'd be campaigning for you at the same time."

Laurie nodded, impressed. "The shirts could be in really hot shades, with a drawing, and something like 'Vote Laurie In' in big, flashy letters."

"Great! And don't make too many of them, so that having one would become a status kind of thing."

"We could give one to all the kids who help in the campaign, too," Laurie added.

Gloria shook her head. "I don't think so. People don't have enough respect for freebies. But what if we let them buy a special edition of the shirt with STAFF printed on the back? They'd all want one, and probably wear them every day, even after the election."

"That's really good thinking, Gloria," said Laurie. "I like your ideas a lot. Hey, have you had lunch yet? What do you say we pick up something and talk a little longer? I've just had an idea of my own about the campaign, and I'd really like to get your reaction to it."

Chapter
6

A Day for Remembering

by Sasha Jenkins

Most of us think of Memorial Day as nothing more than a three-day weekend that marks the official start of summer. It means that the beaches are open, and school is about to close.

Sasha looked up from the typewriter and stared out the window. Since lunchtime clouds had moved in from the west, and were steadily darkening. She tried to remember if she had left her poncho in her locker. If it wasn't there, she might get very wet on the way to her parents' bookstore.

There was no one around to borrow an umbrella from. Friday was publication day for *The Red and the Gold,* the student paper at Kennedy

High, and as usual the rest of the staff was taking the day off. Sasha generally disliked the emptiness of the room on Friday afternoons, but this week she welcomed the silence. She wanted to do some serious writing, without the pressure of looming deadlines.

She had gotten the idea for the column from her boyfriend Wes. Leesburg Academy, where Wes was a cadet, had an award-winning drill team that was scheduled to march in the local Memorial Day parade this year, just as it had done year after year. But this year, according to Wes, some of the members were asking the school to pull the team out of the parade.

"They're not unpatriotic," he had explained, in his soft Virginia drawl. "Not a bit, but they think the parade has turned into a joke. Last year, besides our drill team, there was a little kids' drum and bugle corps, one fire engine, and fifty or sixty veterans in the parade. There were more folks marching than watching. Of course," he added, a little bitterly, "it was a real nice day last year. You can't expect folks to give up their picnics and backyard barbecues just for the sake of a little patriotism, can you?"

"People have different ways of showing their patriotism," Sasha said. "Going to a parade and cheering for whatever the government is doing isn't the only one. There's trying to get the country to do what you think is right, for instance; I call that patriotism, too."

Sasha's mom and dad were committed activists who had taken her to her first protest march when she was still in a stroller. Now that she was

52

older, she found herself disagreeing with some of their ideas, but she still shared their general point of view. Wes, the son of a career Navy officer, had a lot of trouble with that fact about her and her family, just as she and her parents had trouble with his military background and views.

"I don't want to get into that now," he replied. "Anyhow, I'm not talking about showing your love of your country in different ways. I'm talking about not showing it at all. If you told me you wanted to hold a protest sign at the parade, I might not like it much. In fact, I'd probably tell you it was a rotten idea. Still, I think I'd realize that you were showing some kind of concern. Most people these days don't think, or care, one way or the other."

"They've forgotten what Jefferson said: 'Eternal vigilance is the price of liberty.' "

"That's right," Wes said emphatically. " 'Eternal vigilance'. . . . That's the reason we should all give as much support as we can to our armed forces."

"Hmm," said Sasha. "Actually," she added with a touch of slyness, "I think what Jefferson meant is that if citizens want to hold onto their freedom, they have to keep a very sharp eye on what their government does."

He turned pink and took a deep breath, as if about to launch into an argument, but then he suddenly relaxed and gave her a grin that melted her heart. "Your point, I guess," he said. "Have you been keeping score?"

She smiled back. "Not really, but I think it's love-fifteen."

"You're close," he said, reaching for her. "The love part is right, anyway."

The discussion hadn't gotten much further after that, but it did leave Sasha with the theme for her column. She would have plenty of time to write and polish it before the deadline for the last issue in May. Even so, she wanted to get as much of it down as possible while her inspiration was fresh.

But is that really all it means? It used to be called Decoration Day. The name sounds like a joke, until we find out that our grandparents decorated graves on that day.

First it was the Civil War dead who were honored. Then, as war followed war, the meaning of the holiday was expanded to include the piled-up dead from each new conflict.

Maybe it is time to expand its meaning still more, to include not only those who died in our country's foreign wars, but those who fought to keep our land true to its own spirit and dream. Not all of those who died for liberty and justice were in uniform at the time. In fact, some died at the hands of men who *did* wear our country's uniform even as they betrayed its promise.

Those men and women, true freedom fighters, deserve to be remembered just as much as those who served in the armed forces of the nation. This Memorial Day, let us all spare a moment from the volleyball game and the hot dogs on the grill to think of them with gratitude and wonder.

Sasha rolled the page out of the machine and read it over. She needed to do some research among her parents' books, to find just the right

54

examples to illustrate her points, but she liked the way the article flowed. Sometimes being a journalist had its rewards!

A slight frown marred her delicate features as she wondered whether to show the column to Wes and her parents before it was printed. In a sense they deserved to see it because each of them had helped inspire it, but a shrinking sensation in her stomach told her it would not be that simple. She could imagine her father gently asking her if she needed to glorify war and killing, just as she could imagine her stammering attempts to answer. As for Wes, he firmly believed putting on an army or navy uniform changed a person into a different, and better, sort of being. He was not going to —

Someone grabbed her upper arms from behind and held her in her chair. A smacking sound approached her left ear. She jerked her head to the right just in time to avoid a noisy kiss.

"How's my favorite little fox?" a nasal voice asked. "Huh, huh. You getting tired of soldier boy yet?"

"For the last time, John, I am not your little fox, and I do not like you pawing me." She slipped out of his loosened grip and stood up. The burly wrestler was leering at her with eyes so tiny they approached the vanishing point.

"I like my foxettes coy," Marquette replied. "Where's the fun in chasing someone who won't run?"

"Do you want something, John? I have a lot of work to do."

"Of course I want something, little fox. I want to do you a big favor."

"I don't need any favors, thanks," Sasha quickly replied.

"Maybe you don't right this minute, but things can change pretty fast. Take the ads from Superjock, for instance. My cousin, he could decide tomorrow to spend that money some other way, and where would that leave your little newspaper, Jenkins?"

Sasha didn't like the way he called her by her last name, but it was a big improvement over "foxette." She was also beginning to wish she had never heard of Superjock. Every time John Marquette wanted something from the newspaper, which was fairly often, he held his cousin's large ad budget over Sasha's head. "It would leave us in a hole," she replied seriously, "but we'd get out of it somehow. Superjock isn't our only advertiser."

"Naw, just the biggest, that's all. But that wasn't why I came here. I came to give you a scoop. Guess who's running for president of the student body?"

Sasha laughed. "That's stale news, John. Chris told me herself yesterday afternoon."

"Austin?" he said, curling his thick lips into a sneer. "Give me a break! She's such a straight arrow, she hasn't figured out how to turn corners yet!"

Sasha resisted an impulse to ask why turning corners was such an important skill, and asked, "Then who are you talking about? I haven't heard about any other candidates."

56

With a smile that narrowed his eyes still further, he tapped his thumb against his barrel chest.

"*You're* running for president?!" Sasha exclaimed.

"You got it, foxette. Pretty impressive, huh? 'President Marquette' — yeah, I like the sound of that."

"But John," she said weakly, "you're not — "

"I'm not part of the SG crowd, is that what you were going to say? Right, that's the whole point. See, I figure that this school has been run too long by a bunch of preppies and wimps. All they care about is making a record that'll help them get into some fancy ivy-league college."

Sasha winced. In her opinion Brad Davidson had been a solid president, but he had never tried to hide his hope that the post would be a plus with the Princeton admissions committee.

"Kennedy High has a rep.," he continued. "People out there have heard of us. But you know why? You know what put this dump on the map?"

"Well, we're pretty good academically," Sasha began, "and events like the Follies and the *Vogue/GQ* show draw a lot of attention — "

"Wrong. What people notice is that our football team wins the district title every year, and our wrestling team made the state finals, and the girls' track team is one of the best around. *Sports,* that's what gets publicity. But do the people in student government know that, or care? They can find the money to send a chartered bus to some museum, but what happened when we wanted to take a busload of kids to watch an important track meet?"

"It was too late in the term," Sasha recalled. "Student council said that they had already committed all the money they had."

"Sure," John growled. "Well, listen, when I'm president, I'll figure out how to *uncommit* it if something important comes up. We've been shortchanged and dumped on too long by a bunch of dopes who think that only boneheads care about sports. Maybe they're right, but I'm going to show them that there are an awful lot of us boneheads around here."

Sasha found herself wondering if he didn't have a good point. She didn't much care about sports one way or the other, but she knew how important they were to a lot of students. Maybe they weren't being fairly represented by the people in student government. There was material for a good piece of investigative journalism there.

"So there's your scoop," John said, moving toward her. "How about a little reward?"

Sasha quickly put the desk between them. Experience had taught her that it wasn't easy to get out of John's grasp; it was much simpler to stay out of reach. "Thanks for dropping by and telling me," she said. "But you know, this week's issue of the paper is already out, and the next one won't appear until next Friday. We'll be doing a lot of coverage of the campaign in that one."

"Yeah? How about interviewing me for it?" He gave her an exaggerated wink.

Sasha tried to conceal her shudder. The last time she had interviewed Marquette had been a nightmare. He had insisted on doing the interview over dinner, and she finally agreed. All her friends warned her that he was a total animal, but she was sure that she could outsmart him and avoid any real trouble. In the end, all that saved her was the fact that he drank too much vodka on top of too much beer, and passed out. The only concrete damage was a torn sleeve on her new dress, which was easily repaired.

"Our reporters will be talking to all the candidates," she said carefully. "Someone will get in touch with you early next week. Now, if you don't mind, I still have some work to do before — "

"Sure, little fox, sure. But listen, you better not mess up with this interview the way you did the last one. And what about that picture of me, the one from the match where I stomped Forsyte and took the title? Maybe you could run it next to the interview. That'd get me the girls' vote, all right, huh, huh!"

A mad notion crossed Sasha's mind. Somewhere in the photo files was a picture of a huge steer that the National Beef Council had sent to the paper as part of an advertisement. It was quite a sight: a small head, tiny eyes, and a ton or two of pure beef. What if that picture accidentally replaced John's in the paper? A smile touched her lips as she wondered if anyone would notice the mistake.

"Yeah, you remember that picture, don't you, foxette?" John asked, misinterpreting her expression. "Tell you what, you make sure it gets into the paper, and maybe Superjock will need a two-page spread to advertise its summer specials.

59

Who knows? If I get elected, my cousin might even decide to take out two pages in every issue from now on to the end of the term. What do you think of that?"

Sweet, fragile, romantic Sasha Jenkins clenched her fists and turned bright red. "I think it's the most disgusting of all the disgusting things you've ever said, John Marquette," she said in a strong voice. "As long as I'm editor, *The Red and the Gold* is not for sale, to you or anybody! And if you and your precious cousin don't like it, you can both take a hike. We'll get along just fine without you!"

"Hey, you're pretty lively when you're mad," he replied with a grin. "What's so bad about doing a favor or two for somebody who's done a favor for you? But I'll tell you what, you see to it that I get lots of play in the paper, and I'll make sure my cousin *doesn't* take out a bigger ad. How's that, sweet thing?"

Sasha almost laughed at John's strange logic. The anger drained out of her, to be replaced by tiredness. She would never persuade someone like him, or even manage to get him to understand, what she was concerned about. Why bother to try? "Stop worrying," she said. "We'll give you and all the other candidates fair treatment, no more and no less. We don't play favorites.

"Now will you please go away?" she added. "I want to finish what I'm doing, and get out of here before the storm breaks."

Chapter
7

On her way to the parking lot, Laurie stopped by her locker to pick up the newest prize of her wardrobe — a waist-length jacket of pale gray UltraSuede. She had spent a long time finding the right style, fit, and color, and longer still finding a pair of soft ankle boots to match. But it was worth the time and the money to have something that stood out so noticeably in the halls of Kennedy High.

She idly rubbed her cheek against the collar of the coat and purred over her accomplishments of the day. Not only had she filled her petition with hardly any effort; she had even begun to plan her campaign and had found the perfect person to run it.

Gloria hadn't wanted to take the job. She claimed she didn't have enough experience and tried to convince Laurie to get an upperclassman who knew more people and had some background in student politics. But Laurie convinced her that she didn't want someone who was part of the establishment. It was time for fresh, new approaches, and that meant fresh, new faces as well. Once Gloria agreed, they spent the rest of lunch talking over ideas, and making lists of things to do.

Gloria was very emphatic on one point. "We've just got to find out more about Westergard," she said. "What does he really stand for? Who's backing him? What are his weak points, things we can attack him on?"

"I don't know," Laurie said hesitantly. "Do we have to attack him at all? Why don't we just ignore him and tell people what *we* stand for? Once they see and hear him, everyone'll realize he's a nerd and decide to support me."

"We can't count on that. Besides, you can bet that someone from his campaign is busy nosing around for dirt on you right now. We need to have ammunition on hand to fight back."

"I haven't done anything I'm ashamed of," Laurie said uneasily.

"Of *course* you haven't, but you know how stories can get twisted. All I'm saying is that we should be ready for them, in case they start fighting dirty. That doesn't mean we have to fight dirty ourselves. If they know we're prepared, it might keep them from even starting."

Something about Gloria's proposal bothered Laurie. If each side knew the other was ready to start slinging mud, wasn't that likely to make both of them go ahead — to keep the other side from getting the upper hand? They might even get into a battle by accident, because one side *thought* the other had attacked.

When she tried to explain this, however, she couldn't make Gloria see her point. "We have to be prepared for anything," she kept repeating, and in the end, Laurie went along.

That had been their only disagreement. They talked about T-shirts, buttons, leaflets, and posters, and found they were thinking exactly alike. What really counted was *style*, because that was the quality Laurie had and the typical student politicians lacked. They would plaster Laurie's image all over Kennedy High — no, all over Rose Hill — because the image told what the campaign was about.

When Gloria remarked that printed posters and leaflets would cost a lot, Laurie reassured her. She would find the money. Running for school office couldn't cost much more than a couple of designer outfits, and it was certain to be cheaper than a summer in Scandinavia!

Before separating, they agreed to call a meeting for volunteers early the next week. The sooner they got the campaign rolling, the more stunning their victory would be. As Gloria said that, Laurie thought of Lars. Everywhere he went, he would see her face. Then he would hear that the girl he had deceived and abandoned had just won by the biggest margin in the history of Kennedy High School. Too late he would realize what a fool he had been. She wouldn't rub it in, of course. She didn't want to be nasty. When they passed each other in the hall, she would smile sweetly and say hello. If he asked her out, though, she would have to tell him that her new duties didn't leave her time for idle socializing.

A bright flash and an immediate, deafening clap of thunder started her back to the present. She had been standing by her locker daydreaming for too long. The storm, which had been looming all afternoon, was catching up with her. No matter how she hurried, she would never get home before it broke.

Not that she was in such a huge rush to get home. Her dad was in New York for the day, and wouldn't be back until late. All she could look forward to was another warmed-over casserole in a big, empty house. Still, even that beat standing around in the hallway of a big, empty high school.

As she reached the exit nearest the parking lot, the first fat drops of rain began to make craters in the dusty flowerbeds along the walk. She didn't dare run in her new boots, so she held her books over her head, and walked as quickly as she could to the Mustang. All she could think of were her boots. If they got wet, they would be ruined.

Naturally, the car keys were hiding under everything else at the bottom of her purse. But she eventually found them, and managed to open the door. She tossed her books into the backseat, got in, and slammed the door. Her breath immediately began to fog the windshield. Now that she needed it, the rag that usually stayed under her seat was nowhere around. Muttering, she cranked her window down two or three inches, and leaned across to do the same on the passenger side. The breeze helped, as long as she ignored the raindrops that came in as well.

"Come on, sweetie," she murmured, as she started to turn the ignition key. "There's a nice, warm garage waiting for you." The Mustang didn't like the rain, and sometimes it simply refused to move until the weather dried up. Laurie wasn't superstitious, but a couple of times when she had talked nicely to the car, it started right up. Now she did it habitually. It might not help, but it certainly couldn't hurt.

Rrrr. Rrrrrr. Rrrrrrrrr.

That wasn't the starter! Laurie quickly released the ignition key, but the laboring, grinding noise continued. It sounded like a mechanical monster tearing itself apart. But she couldn't identify where it was coming from.

Suddenly she knew: It was the motor that operated the top! But the front edge of the top was still clamped firmly to the windshield. The dealer had warned her when she first got the car, *never* to start the top motor without loosening the clamps. He hadn't said exactly what would happen if she did, whether the top would tear, or the windshield would break, but he had looked very solemn.

The noise continued and seemed to grow louder. She turned the key both ways, but that didn't help at all. With crisp decisiveness she reached up and unsnapped the two clamps. Slowly, majestically, the canvas top rose into the air, folded itself neatly, and disappeared into the space behind the backseat.

At the same moment the rain went from a

sprinkle to a downpour. First the street, next the parking lot, then even the front of the car vanished behind the wavering gray curtain. Laurie's hair flopped heavily over her eyes, and an icy streamlet began to find its way down the inside of her blouse from the base of her neck, along her spine, to her waist.

She gasped for breath and started to shiver. When she turned the ignition key again, the engine started at once, but she was almost too bewildered to notice. No matter how she pushed, pulled, or twisted the switch that was supposed to operate the top, it did nothing at all. Frantic now, and soaked through, she began to push buttons and turn switches completely at random. The headlights flashed, the horn beeped, and the Pink Floyd tape in the cassette deck blared at high volume, but the top stayed where it was.

Tears of anger and frustration mingled with the rain streaming down her face. She began to pound her clenched fists against the steering wheel.

"Hi, there," a cheerful voice said. "Need any help?" A boy in a yellow slicker was leaning over the passenger side door, grinning at her.

"Of course not," she almost said. "I needed a shower anyway!" But she knew this boy was her only hope, so she bit back the words and nodded dumbly. He reached over to unlatch the door, got into the passenger seat, then scrunched down and put his head under the dashboard.

At least he's keeping his head dry, Laurie thought. She felt a flash of resentment at his apparent competence, but it dissolved into gratitude an instant later when the top motor abruptly began to purr. She had never noticed before what an eternally long time the top took to rise into place. Eventually it came to rest against the windshield, and she hurriedly fastened the clamps.

Her rescuer wriggled out from under the dash and sat up. Laurie pushed the wet hair off her face and took a good look at him. He seemed about six feet tall, a bit shorter than Lars, but with broader shoulders and a narrower waist. His face echoed the shape of his body, broad in the forehead and narrowing to a chin that had a Kirk Douglas-type cleft in it. His brown eyes, behind big aviator glasses, seemed both knowing and tolerant.

Closer inspection revealed that the boy was as bedraggled as a puppy that had fallen into the bathtub. When he lifted his arm to wipe his glasses, water streamed out of the turned-up cuff of his sleeve and poured onto his lap. Laurie began to laugh, then realized she was helpless to stop. A moment later she was leaning back in her seat, giggling uncontrollably. After a single startled look, the boy joined in with a deep, rumbling laugh.

As soon as her giggles subsided, Laurie turned off the cassette player, squeezed some of the water out of her hair, and said, "Do I look as funny as you do?"

"Funnier," he replied. "I had a raincoat."

"It didn't do you much good, did it? You're soaked."

"Oh, no, I'm not. There's one spot on my left arm that's totally dry." He rolled up his slicker to show her, but all Laurie saw was a drenched shirt sleeve. "Oops—I mean, that *was* totally dry." As Laurie put the car in gear and started out of the parking lot, he added, "Do I get to find out where we're going, or is this a mystery tour?"

"We're going to my house," said Laurie. "A: I want to be sure that darn top stays up until the car is safe in the garage; and B: I owe you a couple of warm towels, and some hot tea with honey. After that I'll bring you back to school or take you home, whatever you want. Okay?"

"Sure," he said, and settled back in his seat.

At the house, she led him upstairs to her father's dressing room gave him two towels and a big, white terry cloth robe. "Just put your things outside the door," she said. "As soon as I change, I'll take them down and throw them in the dryer."

"Shoes, too?" he asked, moving his feet to produce a loud squishing sound.

She glanced down at the Topsiders, now almost black with wetness, and wrinkled her nose scornfully. "You're on your own there. Why don't you pretend you've been out sailing and the weather turned rough?"

"Aye aye, captain," he retorted, and closed the door.

She took two minutes to get out of her wet clothes and towel off, eight minutes to dry her hair, and at least ten to decide what to put on next. She finally picked a pair of raw silk pants, and a matching top in a soft peach color. She tied a red silk sash at the waist.

Tossing her head back to fluff her hair, she

marched out of her room into the hall. The door to her dad's dressing room was open, and the room was empty. As she stood at the head of the stairs, she thought of the silver in the dining room and wondered if she had let a burglar loose in the house. Then she heard someone whistling a cheery tune from the direction of the kitchen and relaxed. No burglar would go around whistling ragtime.

He was standing next to the stove holding a pile of wet clothes. The terry robe was a good fit. "I thought I'd save you some trouble," he said, "but I can't find the dryer."

"It's this way." She led him through the pantry into the laundry room, tossed the clothes in the dryer, and set it on auto; then she went back to the kitchen and put two cups of water into the microwave. When she looked up, he was grinning at her. His slicked-down hair, beginning to fluff up as it dried, made him look like a little kid. "What's so funny?" she asked defensively.

"Do you always bake your water?"

"It's a lot faster this way. See? It's already hot." She took the cups out and added tea bags. "If you want, I'll heat some in a kettle for you instead," she said mischievously, handing him his tea. "Or you can go out in the yard and rub some sticks together, if the idea of an electric stove upsets you."

"Hey, okay," he laughed. "I surrender! I never saw anyone do it before, that's all. I'm in favor of progress. How fast does that thing make cookies?"

"It doesn't," Laurie admitted. "They don'ᵗ

69

brown the way they're supposed to. We get our cookies in a bag from the supermarket." She located the cookies, spread them on a plate, and carried it into the media room.

He followed her through the doorway, but stopped a few steps into the room. When she looked back, he was shaking his head in amazement. "Wow," he said, "is your dad in electronics?"

"Cable TV," Laurie replied.

"What a system! I've never seen anything like it! Is that a compact disc player over there?"

"Um-hum. It's a new model that plays compact audio discs and LaserVision, too. Want to see?"

She switched on the projection TV. As the screen descended from the ceiling, she hunted for a new music video disk her father had brought home a few days before, and slipped it into the compact disc player. A huge, grotesquely made-up face suddenly blossomed on the screen, perfectly synched with the roaring voice from the two concealed speakers.

Her new friend watched and bit his lower lip in astonishment, then turned to say something. She hit the mute button. In the sudden silence, he said, "Amazing — it's like having your own theater, isn't it? It's so overwhelming, though. I don't think I could take much of it at a time."

Laurie shrugged and turned off the video. His enthusiasm for all her father's gadgets was starting to bore her. He had paid attention to every piece of electronic gear in the room, but hadn't so much as glanced at her outfit. "You get used to it," she said, yawning.

"I guess so." He came close and took a cookie from the plate.

Her pulse beat a little faster. "Is that all you want?" she asked in a provocative voice.

He smiled crookedly, deepening the dimple in his chin. "For now," he said.

She slowly backed away, until her calves touched the edge of the couch. "Why don't we sit down and get to know each other better?" she continued. "I'm Laurie Bennington."

"I know," he replied, taking the seat next to her. "I'm Dick Westergard."

Chapter 8

"Dick Westergard? *You?*" Laurie stared at the tall, handsome boy in the terry cloth robe, as if she thought he might suddenly transform himself into the wimpy techno-freak she had imagined him to be. He seemed to guess her thoughts, and find them very funny.

"Uh-huh," he said breezily, "himself, in person. The next vice-president of Kennedy High School — unless you beat me, of course."

"Beat you? You bet I'm going to beat you," Laurie proclaimed. "And I don't think it was very nice of you to come around spying on me like that, either. If that's the kind of campaign you're going to run, you'll find out that two can play that game!"

He held both hands up, palms out. "Hey, wait a minute, wait a minute! What's all this spying jazz? As I recall I was running across the parking lot trying to beat the rain, I saw you were having trouble, and came over to see if I could help. But

72

maybe you remember differently?"

"Well. . . ."

"And then you kidnapped me, brought me to your hideout, and took away all my clothes," he continued. He gave her an infuriating grin, and made a big deal of tucking the robe more tightly around his neck. "I suppose the next step in your sinister plan is to torture me into revealing the secret plans for my victory."

There was something so impish in his expression, Laurie couldn't help grinning back and falling in with his game. "Where are the plans?" she demanded in a menacing voice. "You must give me the plans."

"Never! Do your worst, colonel, I'll never tell!"

"We have ways of making you talk," she said in a heavy Late Show accent.

"Nuts! We Americans are tough. Nothing you can do will make me talk."

"So? You think not? What if I play a Barry Manilow video with the sound turned off?"

He shook his head scornfully.

"Indeed. You leave me no choice, then. I shall play the Barry Manilow video with the sound turned ON!"

He instantly fell on his knees and clasped his arms around her ankles, pleading, "No, no, anything but that! I'll tell you! I'll tell you!"

"Stop that, you goof! You're going to trip me!" She tried to back away, but found it hard to move while he was holding her ankles. "Come on, let me go. Let go, I said!"

Fighting back an attack of giggles, she jerked one foot loose and tried to hop out of his ridiculous embrace. Too late she remembered the last time she had done any serious hopping had been in fifth grade. She hadn't been terribly good at it, even then. By now she was even worse. The hop became a topple, and she found herself lying on the rug with her head only inches from the leg of the sofa.

"Are you all right?" he asked, crawling hastily over beside her.

The back of her head ached where it had struck the floor, but it didn't seem to be the sort of pain that needed attention. Lying flat on the floor like that was strangely relaxing, and she felt no desire to sit up.

"Laurie? Are you okay?"

The concern was written so plainly on his face that she wanted to reassure him. She reached up, placed one hand on each side of his face, and pulled him toward her. After a fleeting moment of confusion his expression became determined, though a hint of nervousness flickered around the edges. Just as she closed her eyes, she saw his face moving to hers.

Then his lips met and joined hers. Surprised by their softness, she relaxed her grip on his head. He, in turn, slipped an arm under her neck and pulled her closer to him. She wrapped her arms around him, and ran her hands down the long muscles on either side of his spine. A dreamy warmth spread through her body. She never wanted to move again.

"Laurie," he whispered, "Laurie, we'd better. . . ."

Dick pulled away from her, and the moment

ended as suddenly as it had begun. Disappointment raced through her, followed closely by rage. She sat up and looked around for something to throw, only to be overcome by a tremendous sneeze.

"Bless you," he said.

"Thank — " She broke off the polite reply to cover her face against another monster sneeze. When she blinked the tears from her eyes, she discovered him standing next to her holding out a tissue. She took it, dabbed at her face, and said, "I think I caught cold."

"So do I. Do you want me to bake you some more tea, with lemon and honey?"

She nodded mutely. As he left the room, she began to ask herself what had just happened. She hadn't *meant* to make a play for him, she was sure of that. This was the boy who was running against her. He was a member of the chess team and the Computer Club. But he certainly wasn't a nerd.

Laurie frowned as she thought of how quickly and easily he had pulled away from her. Then Gloria's warnings about dirty politics flooded her brain. Perhaps this was part of a trick to get her to reveal information about her campaign.

If that was Dick's game, Laurie could certainly play. Maybe it was time to start gathering information on him. Laurie laughed; she knew she was kidding herself. Her attraction to Dick was real, and campaign spying was just an excuse to see more of him. But she had no way of knowing what Dick's real motives were.

Dick reappeared carrying two steaming mugs

of tea, and Laurie allowed herself to forget her suspicions. He was wearing his jeans and plaid shirt again, though his feet were still bare. "Rumpled but dry," he said as he handed her her tea. "I decided to let the socks take a few more spins. Oh, and I left the robe by the washer. Is that okay?"

"Sure. Mrs. Byrne will take care of it on Monday," Laurie said. "She's the housekeeper," she added in response to his look of curiosity.

"Oh. Is your mother. . . ." he began cautiously.

"She and Daddy have been divorced since I was ten," Laurie said. She spoke as if she were repeating a well-rehearsed speech. "She lives in Pacific Palisades, California. That's near Los Angeles. I used to live with her out there, but her new husband has three kids of his own. We didn't get along very well, so I decided to come live with Daddy."

"Oh." He sat down near her on the curved sofa and took a sip of his tea. "Do you miss California?"

"I miss the ocean a lot," she replied. "I used to spend all the time I could on the beach. Oh, and I used to love driving up into the mountains early in the morning. The mountains are right there, you know, just ten or fifteen minutes away."

He shook his head. "The farthest west I've ever been was visiting my great-grandmother in St. Louis. I'd like to see the Rockies, and the desert, and all that, some day."

"I can show you what it's like where I lived, if you want. Some people filmed a video there, at the beach and up in the foothills." She went over

76

to the shelves of cassettes. She knew exactly where to find the one she wanted. "The music is pretty crummy, though, so I usually play it with the sound off."

"I get it," he laughed, "silent videos, like silent movies. I should have made popcorn instead of tea."

Laurie paused with the cassette in her hand. "Do you want some popcorn? We can make it in the microwave in about half a minute."

"No, that was a joke."

"Oh." The VCR swallowed the cassette, and she took the remote control back to the sofa. "A couple of kids I knew were extras in this," she said, as the camera tracked along a deserted stretch of beach, faster and faster, toward a distant clump of people. "In a minute they'll focus on a guy with a blond Mohawk, wearing a green shirt. That's Tim Dawson — there, see?"

"I guess so," Dick said. "He wasn't on the screen very long."

"Maybe not, but it gave his career a huge boost. Would you believe that he shaved his head right before the auditions? He's not really punk at all, but he knew that was what they were looking for."

"He gained the part by losing his part," Dick said with a grin. When she didn't respond, he bent his head down and tapped the part in his hair. "Sorry," he added, "dumb joke. The ocean is beautiful, but the hills are pretty bleak, aren't they? Not like around here at all."

"No, but I miss them sometimes, just the same. Would you like to watch anything else? There's

77

all kinds of stuff on cassette and laser disk both. We can phone for a pizza later." Her manner was so offhand and casual, she was sure he couldn't sense the tension underneath.

"I wish I could," he began.

Her heart sank. "The thing is," he continued, "I have to get home pretty soon. I'm baby-sitting for my two sisters this evening."

"Really? How old are they?"

"Melissa is eight, and Anne is ten. Say, you wouldn't like to come help, would you? I could really use it."

"Come on, you ought to be able to take care of two little girls on your own." Laurie had regained enough of her composure not to appear overly enthusiastic.

"Oh sure. But the fact is, they're both having friends over on sleep-overs. My scientific observations indicate that two little girls are four times as hard to handle as one, so by extrapolation, four will be sixteen times as hard. We can still have pizza," he added, looking at her hopefully.

Laurie laughed. "And spend the rest of the night cleaning mozzarella and tomato sauce off them? Give me a break!"

"Does that mean you'll come? Terrific!"

She hadn't actually decided to do it, but the pleasure on his face made her mind up for her. "I'll go put on something more practical," she said. "I'll just be a minute. You'd better get your socks out of the dryer before they shrivel up completely."

It took her a good deal longer than a minute to change. She looked over her choices with as much care as if she was going to the party of the year, balancing sexy against homey, and both against comfortable and fashionable. Finally, she settled for overdyed baggy jeans; a wide-necked French sailor's jersey, cinched at the waist with a wide belt; and ballet slippers.

Dick was waiting at the bottom of the stairs, grinning. "I hope you remember what stores all your things come from," he said. "Anne is sure to ask. She is a total nut about clothes."

"We'll have a lot to talk about, then," Laurie said.

As they were going out the back door, he asked, "Aren't you going to leave a note saying where you'll be?"

"I'm free to come and go as I please," she replied with a mixture of pride and defensiveness.

"Oh sure," he said quickly. "I only meant — never mind." He glanced up at the sky, and in an obvious change of subject said, "Are you going to put the top down?"

Laurie laughed grimly. "Not if I can help it!"

Two hours later Laurie found herself sitting patiently on the floor of the Westergards' living room, while Melissa and her friend Debbie used up half a container of hair mousse to pull Laurie's hair into one shape after another. Across the room, Dick was just holding his own against the two older girls in a fierce game of dominoes. She caught his eye and smiled.

"I'd trade places with you," he called, "but they don't *want* to do my hair. Tell them that's illegal sex discrimination, will you?"

"Tell them yourself," she retorted. "You just want a way to get out of that game without having to admit that you're losing."

"Losing? What are you talking about? I'm deliberately going easy on them."

"Yaaahh!" his sister Anne said, pinching his arm. "You always say that whenever I beat you at anything."

"Uh huh, and whenever I beat *you*, you always say it's not fair."

"Well, it isn't," she replied with unshakable logic. "You're a lot bigger than me."

He grinned and shook his head ruefully at Laurie. "An answer for everything. Were you like than when you were ten?"

Laurie was silent. When she was ten, her mom and dad were getting their divorce. She still wondered occasionally if she could have done anything to prevent it. Back then she had been sure she could, if only she was smart enough, or good enough, or lucky enough, to figure out what to do.

"There," Melissa said, breaking into her thoughts. "We're done. Come and look." She took Laurie's left hand, her friend took the right, and together they pulled her to her feet and out to the mirror in the front hall. "What do you think?" Melissa asked anxiously.

Laurie managed to keep a straight face. The girls had made three fountains of hair in a line along the left side of her head and tied pieces of red ribbon into them. Her first thought was that it made her head so lopsided she was in danger of tipping over. Her second was that she had actually seen a similar hairstyle somewhere before, although she couldn't imagine where.

Then she remembered, and she *did* crack up. Just before she left California, a classmate had taken her to an exhibition of show jumping and dressage. Many of the horses had ribbons braided into their manes in exactly this fashion. She widened her nostrils and was about to toss her head, then noticed that the girls were still waiting for her reaction.

"If you don't like it," Debbie said, "we can do it another way. We've got loads of ideas."

"I'll bet you do. But I think I'll leave it just like this. It's *very* original. Would you like me to do yours now?"

They immediately handed her the comb and brush and tugged her back to the sofa.

Mr. and Mrs. Westergard got home a few minutes after ten and took over. They pretended to be shocked that the girls were still up. Laurie smiled to herself; from her recollections of grade-school sleep-overs, she bet that they would still be up whispering to each other at three in the morning.

Dick walked her out to her car. "Thanks," he said softly. "You were a real help. The girls loved having you here. So did I."

"I had fun," she said simply. She looked up at him, not quite smiling, and waited. Slowly he bent his head down toward her. His hands touched her waist so lightly, she might have been imagining it. As if they were two magnets, she found herself swaying in his direction just as he was moving in hers. Then his arms were around her and his lips were on hers, and the rushing sound in her ears blotted out the night noises around them.

Too soon, she made herself pull back and say, "I'd better go." But just saying that used up all her resolve. She nestled closer and rested her head on his chest. Beneath her ear, his heart was pounding loudly, and she thought how strange that something so unknowable should be only inches away.

"Laurie?" he said.

"Um?"

"Nothing." His arms tightened around her. "I just felt like saying your name."

"I'd better go," she repeated. "Your folks will be wondering what happened to you."

"That's funny," he said, "*I'm* wondering what happened to me."

"Me, too. I can guess, though." She tilted her face up for another kiss, then backed away and got into the car.

He leaned on the door. "I'll see you in school on Monday."

"Okay." She started the engine. Monday seemed like a very long way away. "Sleep well."

"You, too." He put his head inside the car and kissed her again quickly, on the cheek. Then he walked away. Just as a feeling of desolation was starting to wash over her, he turned at the door and waved. Warmed and reassured, she waved back and drove toward home. She was no longer concerned about the election. Somehow, she knew, everything would work itself out.

Chapter *9*

After lunch on Sunday Phoebe changed into a halter, an old pair of cutoffs, and flip-flops. She tied a bandanna around her head, and went out to work in the garden. Weeding had been on her list of household duties since she was twelve, but this year it was more than just another chore.

In December her parents had asked her to take over most of the responsibility for the garden, and she had agreed. The first task was to decide what to plant. She had spent several chilly, gray afternoons sitting at the breakfast table, poring over seed catalogs. The colors in the pictures, unbelievable as they were, seemed to brighten the room, and the written descriptions kept her constantly on the edge of hunger.

The more she looked, however, the harder choosing became. At the supermarket it was easy: if you wanted tomatoes, you bought tomatoes. But the seed catalog displayed twenty different varieties of tomatoes, each one described as lusciously as possible. Green beans might be runners, climbers, or bush beans. The grocer never mentioned *that* detail. If her mother bought burpless cucumbers, she certainly never discussed it. She didn't even consider the varieties of squash; last time they tried that, vines had overtaken their backyard and the neighbors' as well.

She finally gave up and asked her mother for help. They sat down together with a pen, a loose-leaf notebook, and the catalogs. They made up their list in two hours. One thing her mom showed her was how to pick varieties of a vegetable that matured at different rates, so they wouldn't be smothered in carrots or tomatoes during one week and going without for the rest of the season. It had never occurred to Phoebe that that might be a problem.

The hardest work, preparing the ground for planting, turned out to be a blessing of sorts. It coincided with the period when she was grounded for her part in wrecking Woody's car. Whenever the frustration of being shut in the house started to get to her, she went out back, and hoed up a few more yards of earth. That had happened pretty often. By planting time, not a clod bigger than a thumbnail had survived.

She threw herself into the business of planting as well. First she drew charts of the garden on graph paper and decided where each vegetable would go. Some of her decisions were practical — plants that grew tall had to be where they wouldn't keep the sun from lower plants — but some were pure whimsy. She placed the carrots near the peas because peas and carrots went together. The lettuce and cucumbers went next to the tomato plants in what she thought of as the salad bar.

The more carefully she placed the seeds, the more meticulously straight she made the rows, the less she thought about Griffin. Those were the days when she didn't know what had happened to him, only that he had told her not to call and then dropped completely out of sight. In her fantasies, she sometimes saw him happily dating a glamorous, sophisticated girl from his show, hardly recalling even the name of the girl he had known so briefly back in Rose Hill. At other times she imagined him lying unconscious and unidentified in the charity ward of a hospital. Both fantasies, and all the variations on them, had one thing in common: They made her miserable. Digging the hole for a tiny young tomato plant to just the right depth kept her from dwelling on these thoughts and kept her reasonably happy.

Now that her seeds were sprouting, the garden was becoming both a routine and a joy. She knelt down on the sun-warmed earth, fork in hand, and loosened the soil around each seedling. She was getting very good at telling what was a weed; at least, she hoped she was. Now and then she still referred to the pictures on the seed packets she had tacked to wooden stakes at the end of each row, and hoped the artist had drawn the leaves accurately.

As she worked, she hummed a song that Sasha had played for her: "Inch by inch, row by row, gonna make this garden grow. . . ."

The sun was hot on her bare back. She was starting to think about putting on suntan lotion, or even a shirt, when her little brother Shawn called her from the back door. "Hey, Pheeb, telephone! It's some guy."

She straightened up and rubbed the small of her back, then shook her left foot, which had fallen asleep. Who would be calling her now? It was probably a kid from one of her classes, wanting to check on the next day's assignment.

She picked up the phone in the kitchen, said hello, then caught her breath as she heard Griffin's voice on the other end.

"What was that?" she asked breathlessly.

"I asked how you're doing," he repeated. "Were you taking a nap?"

"No, I was out in the garden."

"Ah, sunstroke! I knew there was something different about you. Has the rest of you gotten as red as your hair yet?"

"Come see for yourself," Phoebe said daringly.

"Ah, don't I wish I could," he said with a theatrical sigh.

"Griffin? Are you all right?"

"Not bad, not bad at all. In fact, pretty good. My job is as boring as they come, but acting school is very exciting. I never realized how much I have to learn."

"You're a terrific actor," Phoebe insisted.

"Oh, I have talent," he agreed, "but that's not enough to carry me. I need training as well, and that's what I'm beginning to get. The theater is a whole world, Phoebe, and I'm just starting to explore the edges of it."

Phoebe felt a pang of jealousy. This new world had already carried him far away from her. But his next words gave her some reassurance.

"That's one reason I'm calling," he said. "I've been given a part in a week-long showcase at the school. It's not a starring role. But some very influential people come to these performances to look for new faces, and they don't look just at the leads. Besides, it'll be my first time before a real audience since we wowed them at the Kennedy Follies. You remember?"

"I'll never forget it as long as I live!"

"I won't, either," he said in a tone that turned her insides to mush. "I miss you so much, Phoebe. For a few days, part of me was almost sorry I had seen you. It made me remember how much I love you and how sad I am to be away from you."

Tears blurred Phoebe's eyes, and she ached to feel his arms around her again. "Griff — " she began, but she couldn't begin to say what she felt, not on the telephone, not with her kid brother sitting three feet away.

"The showcase is three weeks from now, starting Saturday night and running for a week. I know it's asking a lot, but it would give me such a high to know that you were sitting out there in the audience. If you came for the first performance, we could have a whole weekend together."

She wanted to agree instantly. Any practical problems could wait; the main thing was that he wanted her and was asking her to come. "I'd love to," she said fervently. Then she recalled that her mother was nearby and lowered her voice. "But I'm not sure I can swing it."

"One of the girls in my class has a studio couch in her apartment," he said. "She'll be glad to put you up."

Phoebe felt another pang of jealousy, this time directed more specifically. It wasn't so much the thought of another girl that disturbed her, as was the notion that his life was going on without her, and she knew so little about any of it.

"I'll have to see," she said. "I really want to."

"I really want you to. I'll send you all the details tomorrow. Phoebe?"

"Yes?"

"I love you."

She lowered her voice to a whisper. "I love you, too, Griffin. I'll dream of you tonight."

"I dream of you every night, Phoebe. I'll see you soon."

"Yes," she said, "soon. But not soon enough. Good-bye."

As soon as she said that awful word — good-bye — a hundred things she meant to say came pouring into her mind. But before she could take a breath, there was a click, then a dial tone. Slowly she hung up the receiver, and leaned her forehead against the wall. What was she going to do?

"Are you feeling all right, dear?" her mother said.

"Oh sure." She straightened up. "I was just resting for a minute."

Her mother came across the room and studied her face. "I do believe your nose is getting red," she said. "Here, the sunblock is in the cabinet over here. You don't want to use up your whole allowance of freckles this early in the season. Was that you on the telephone just now?"

This was as close to prying as her mom would let herself get. It was also a good opportunity to explain about Griffin's show, and ask permission to go. After a moment's hesitation, however, Phoebe dodged the issue and said only, "Uh huh. I was talking to a friend." She took the tube of sunblock and applied some to her nose and cheeks. She needed time to think things over before she brought up a plan as controversial as going to New York.

"Oh. Are you going back out to the garden now? I'd wear a shirt and my straw hat, if I were you. This is the worst time of the day for burns, you know."

Phoebe sighed. Her mother could barely stand to let her go into the backyard without a chaperone. She'd never stand for a trip to New York.

Phoebe was coming back downstairs, rolling up the sleeves of one of her dad's old shirts, when an old red Volvo pulled up in front of the house and Woody got out. The sight of him lifted Phoebe's spirits. He could provide a crash course in big city survival. She smiled. As glad as Phoebe was that he and Kim Barrie had become Kennedy's latest couple, she missed having him around all the time. She had always been able to depend upon his humor, and his concern for her.

"Hi," she said when she met him at the door. "I'm working in the garden. Want to help?"

"Sure. Take your pick: moral support or cheering section. I'm first class at both."

"I was thinking more in terms of 'Tote that barge, lift that bale,' " Phoebe replied.

"Sorry, wrong fellow. The guy you want is Old Man River. He lives over next to the canal, unless he's off somewhere 'just rolling along.' "

"Next to the canal?" Phoebe said with a straight face. "Isn't he the one who never locks up when he leaves home?"

"Booo!" Woody made an elaborate gesture of holding his nose. He always pretended to despise Phoebe's attempts at puns, though his own were usually pretty feeble, too. "I'll help if you promise no more jokes," he said.

"Let's go out back. There's something I want to talk to you about. Would you like some lemonade? I think we have some lace cookies left, too."

"Super! Lead on, fair damsel, lead on!"

They set up a couple of folding chairs in the shade of an old maple tree and sat down. For the first five minutes they were both content to enjoy the shade, the light breeze, and the birds chirping overhead. Then Phoebe sat up straighter, and told Woody about the invitation from Griffin. Even before Phoebe mentioned her parents, Woody knew what her problem would be.

"How do your parents like the idea?"

"I don't think they will," she said, brooding about her fate. "I haven't asked them yet."

"Uh huh . . . are you doing to?"

"I don't know. Last fall I was all set to go up there without telling them. I even convinced Chris to cover for me. But then Griff called it off. It was awful, but part of me was relieved. I hated the thought of lying to them. And now, after that whole business with Sasha and Wes, and the cabin — "

"Not to mention my car," Woody interjected.

" — and your car, I hate the idea even more." Phoebe winced just mentioning the episode that had gotten her grounded. She had lent her parents' mountain cabin to Sasha and her boyfriend without permission, only to learn that an important client of her father's was planning to use it. Taking Woody's car, she had rushed up and retrieved Sasha and Wes. On the way home, however, the Volvo wrapped itself around a tree, and they had to be towed all the way to Rose Hill. Phoebe was grounded for a month as a result, and it was almost the end of Sasha and Wes's whole relationship.

"I can't take the chance on something like that happening a second time," she went on. "They'd never trust me again. But I've *got* to get up there for Griffin's performance. He needs me there, I know it. And I need to be with him."

"I understand," Woody said. "Maybe I wouldn't have a few months ago, but now. . . . Well, if Kim moved back to Pittsburgh, I think I'd buy a commuter pass between here and there — if there is such a thing. I couldn't stand not seeing her every day."

"It's awful to feel that way, isn't it?"

"Awful or wonderful. I haven't made up my mind which." He finished his lemonade before adding, "Maybe both."

"That reminds me, where *is* Kim? I couldn't reach her earlier. Do she and her mom have a catering job today?"

He made a face. "Nope. She's over at Chris's house, planning the campaign. They've been at it all day."

"Really? What are they doing?"

"I don't know," he shrugged, "maybe writing position papers, or making lists of possible endorsers to call. For all I know, they're already blowing up balloons for the victory party, if there is one. You've heard the latest, haven't you?"

"About John Marquette running for president?" Phoebe laughed. "Yeah, Sasha told me. What a riot! You're not trying to tell me that Chris is worried about that neckless wonder, are you?"

"You bet she is. But that isn't the latest. Relate to this if you can: One of the candidates for vice-president is none other than Laurie Bennington."

"Really? The original off-the-shoulder girl is running for office? I thought she was too busy with Stockholm's gift to the USA."

"No more, it seems." Woody frowned. "And to my suspicious mind, it seems like too much of a coincidence that both she and Marquette are running for office. You remember the way he leaned on us to get her included in the fashion show. I wouldn't be surprised if they turn out to have hatched a plot to take over the student government at Kennedy. And, I wouldn't be *very* surprised if their plot works!"

Chapter 10

Janie Barstow was the first one at the table. She sat down, took a couple of bites of her salad, and pulled the latest issue of Italian *Vogue* from her knapsack. She really enjoyed looking at it every month. The clothes were fantastic, the photography stunning, and she was even beginning to learn some Italian.

A slight smile crossed her face as she flipped the pages. Three or four months before, the notion that she might take a serious interest in fashion would have seemed utterly ridiculous. She had been the original ugly duckling, creeping around in long skirts and drab, shapeless sweaters, trying to keep people from noticing how tall she was.

Then she met Henry, whose father coached football at Rose Hill State, and stumbled upon his secret: During the afternoons when his dad thought he was at basketball practice, Henry was actually hiding out in the home ec room designing and making women's clothes. To Henry's eye, her height was not a curse but a great asset. Once she saw herself in the dresses he created for her, she had to agree.

Henry's designs had been the sensation of the *Vogue/GQ* Show, especially the evening dress Janie had modeled at the climax of the event. As a result, the owner of Rezato, an exclusive Georgetown boutique, had asked Henry to create a line of dresses for her. The local newspapers had loved the story about the talented teenage designer. It looked as though he was on his way to fame and success before he even finished high school.

Janie had done all she could to help him, and still did. The only problem was that the greater his success, the busier he was, and the busier he was, the less time they had to spend together. She found herself thinking wistfully of the period before the *Vogue/GQ* Show when the two of them had worked late every night in her basement, racing to get the dresses finished in time. They had been constantly tired, but they had enjoyed the struggle.

"Hey, hey," a familiar voice said, "it's Janie the B in person. What's shakin', baby?" Peter Lacey, Kennedy High's own DJ, took the seat across from her and started unwrapping a sandwich.

"Peter," she asked accusingly, "what are you doing here?"

"Eating lunch," he mumbled around a mouthful of ham and cheese.

"But it's lunchtime!"

He swallowed and said, "You know any better time to eat lunch?"

"Your show, silly," she said fondly. "What about your show?"

"Without you beside me, to guide me, I couldn't go on." He clasped both hands over the left side of his battered leather jacket, in a gesture straight from the silent movies.

"Peter," she said, "you've been getting along just fine for months now." Janie had been Peter's assistant at WKND through the fall. But she made the mistake lots of girls made, and developed a very heavy crush on the handsome, dashing Lacey. The complications this created eventually led to her quitting the radio station, and hiding in embarrassment every time she saw Peter in the hall. The fact that she could kid around with him now was another result of the transformation Henry had helped bring about in her.

Peter made a lightning switch to vintage Matt Dillon. "It's, like, the strain, you know. It finally got to me. I couldn't take it, I couldn't take it no more, no *no* . . . !"

"*Cut!*" Jamie spoke as firmly as she could. Peter was perfectly capable of working up to an ear-splitting shriek, right in the middle of the lunchroom. "Let me guess," she added quickly. "Equipment trouble, right?"

"Wrong! Want to try again?"

"Hmm . . . your voice sounds okay; as good as it ever does, anyway — "

"Thanks a bunch!"

" — and as far as I know it isn't some important holiday, like Bruce Springsteen's birthday."

"Nope. You're getting colder."

"So you must have been pre-empted. Or cancelled."

"Pre-empted," he said, and pointed toward the speaker built into the ceiling. Now that she listened, she could hear a male voice speaking, but she couldn't make out the words. "A program on the dangers of drunk driving," Peter explained. "The administration leaned on us to put it on."

"It's a big problem," Janie said.

"It's a lousy radio show," he replied. "If they'd asked me to, I would have put one together that kids would *listen* to. Maybe I'll do that anyway."

"Hey, sure, you really ought to," she enthused. "If it's as good as you expect, you could syndicate it to other school radio stations all over the country. Do some good and make money at the same time."

He laughed. "You've turned into a complete businessperson since you and Henry got together, haven't you? How's he doing?"

"Great. What do you hear from Lisa?"

Lisa Chang, Peter's girl friend, was a champion figure-skater and had won a place for herself at a school in Colorado that groomed potential Olympic contestants. She had been away from Rose Hill since late fall. Janie liked her, and thought she and Peter made a good couple. But she also sensed that the long separation was putting more strain on their relationship than it could stand.

"She's fine," Peter said airily, "keeping busy.

They work the kids pretty hard at that school, you know. It has a strong academic program as well as all the emphasis on sports. Between homework and practicing, she doesn't have a lot of free time."

"Does she get the summer off? Will she be coming back to town?"

"I don't know." He looked up and said, "Hi, Sasha." He sounded relieved to be able to get off the subject of Lisa.

Janie turned around and smiled a greeting. "No yogurt today, Sasha?" she asked. "I'm shocked."

Sasha took Janie's kidding seriously. "The salad looked better than usual," she said. "And to tell you the truth, I get tired of yogurt sometimes. I know how good it is for me, but I'm running out of ideas for healthy things to put in it."

"I know," said Peter with a wicked grin, "how about sliced M&M's and a crumbled-up Twinkie?"

Sasha's face turned pale.

"Peter," Janie said, "behave."

"Yes, ma'am. Well, look who's coming to pay us a call: Kennedy High's *hottest* politician."

His imitation of the way Laurie said her favorite adjective told Janie what to expect. Laurie was apparently abandoning her Swedish folk costumes and going back to the look that had made her famous at school. Her outfit was built around tight white jeans, bright yellow socks, and a yellow sleeveless sweater with no blouse under it.

A cluster of thin rubber bracelets in yellow, orange, and red circled her left wrist, and a bright sunburst dangled from her left ear.

"Hello, you guys," Laurie said. "Can I join you for a few minutes?"

"Why not?" Peter replied coolly, and pulled out a chair for her.

"Janie, I know that must be one of Henry's *fabulous* dresses you're wearing. It looks just exactly right on you. I stopped by Rezato the last time I was in Georgetown, and Miss Wainwright told me that she is incredibly pleased with the designs he did for her. You must be really proud."

Janie nodded mutely and looked down at the table. She normally liked to hear people praise Henry's work, but Laurie's comments embarrassed her.

"Sasha Jenkins," Laurie continued, seemingly unaware of Janie's reaction, "you've let me down! You promised to do more articles like the one on old customs you wrote back around Christmas. That was so interesting, and so original. Every week I pick up *The Red and the Gold* expecting to see a feature by you, but all I find are news stories. I know you have to report the news, and of course, you do it very well, but you're capable of so much more."

"I have a couple of things in the works," Sasha said quietly.

"Oh, I hope so. You could do so much to raise the cultural level of the school. As for you, Peter," she said, turning to him, "I know better than to talk to you about raising the cultural level around here."

He looked hurt. "Hey, I keep students hip to what's really happening in the culture *right now*," he said. "Anybody can tell them what happened hundreds of years ago."

"Only kidding, sweetie," she said, patting his hand. "You know, I really miss the old days — being on the air with you and Janie, hanging around the studio, learning how to use a mike and how to run the control board. We had a lot of fun, didn't we?"

Without waiting for an answer, she sighed and said, "But life can't be all fun, can it? I guess you've heard that I'm running for vice-president."

"Yup," said Peter. Janie and Sasha just nodded.

"I see so much that needs to be done, to bring student government back to the students. I don't think I, nor anyone, can do it all in one short year. But I think it's important to make a start, to set a direction. I know you agree."

Janie glanced quickly at Sasha and Peter, then back at her tray. She was amazed at Laurie's confidence. She seemed to have entirely forgotten the trouble she had caused for Peter and Janie by suggesting to Janie that Peter really cared for her. She also seemed to have forgotten that after praising Sasha's feature stories, she had accused her of unfairness and bad reporting in her news stories.

"I've done what I can as student activities officer," Laurie continued. "Having a regular radio spot to talk about what SG was up to was a good example. For a while, I think I managed to get people more interested, and more involved. But

I guess I stepped on a few too many important toes in the process. The next thing I knew, I was off the air. That couldn't have happened if I'd been an elected officer, instead of being appointed by student council."

"I thought you gave up your radio show on your own," Sasha said.

"Lots of people thought that," Laurie replied in a dark voice. "Some people found it very convenient to let the student body think that."

"Like who?" Peter enquired.

"I don't want to get into name calling. That's all history now, anyway. What matters is that as vice-president I'm going to be the truly independent voice of the students. But to get elected, I'm going to need the help of everyone who agrees with my goals. That's why I wanted to talk to you guys, to let you know what I plan to do, and to ask for your support."

A long awkward silence followed. Finally Sasha said, "I don't think I ought to take a position, Laurie. *The Red and the Gold* will probably make endorsements, but as a reporter I think I ought to stay neutral."

"I understand," Laurie said in a disappointed voice.

"Yeah," said Peter, "well, I'm pretty much with Sasha on that. If I go around endorsing candidates, people might think my news stories are slanted or something."

"I see. Janie? You're not a reporter; what do you say?"

"I don't know," Janie said, wishing she could hide under the table. "I think student government ought to be more open, too, but I haven't heard all the issues yet. Besides, I already promised Kim that I'd support Chris."

"Chris is running for president," Laurie said in a tight voice. "I'm running for vice-president."

"Oh sure, I know, but. . . ." She trailed off into silence.

"I see," Laurie repeated. She pushed her chair back and stood up. "Well, it's been good to talk to all of you. I'll be seeing you around."

As she stalked off, Ted Mason appeared from the other direction and took the seat she had just vacated. "What did *she* want?"

"Our endorsements and support," Sasha replied.

He gave a low whistle. "She has a lot of nerve, doesn't she?"

"I don't know," Sasha said, "I got the feeling she really expected us to support her. She seemed awfully disappointed when we didn't."

"That's right," Janie added. "It's as if she doesn't remember any of the things she's done in the past."

"Maybe she thinks *we* don't remember them," Peter said.

Janie's cheeks reddened and she carefully avoided Peter's eye. Laurie had talked Janie into believing Peter wanted to take her to the homecoming dance as a date. In fact, all he had asked her to do was help him with the music. He had already had a date for the dance — Lisa. She still didn't know whether Laurie had acted out of ignorance or malice, but either way, she didn't like her much.

"Look out," Ted said. "Little Laurie never does anything without a reason. She knows you're friends of Chris and Brenda, so how could she have really expected you to support her? Peter, remember the way she tried to use your radio show to keep Chris from becoming homecoming princess? And the way she bad-mouthed Brenda every chance she got? She has to know you're about as likely to support her as you are to support a crocodile. So why did she ask? What does she think she can get out of it?"

Peter furrowed his brow. "Maybe," he said slowly, "maybe she asks me and Sash to endorse her, right? Then when we don't, she comes back that KND and *The Red and the Gold* are prejudiced against her. We're trying to rig the election. So everyone votes for her because they think she's being picked on."

"Not just her, either," Sasha said. "You know who's running against Chris, don't you? And isn't Laurie a good friend of Marquette's? I bet they planned this whole thing together."

"Sure," Peter continued, "that's why she kept going on about cliques running the school. She's going to say we're all members of some kind of sinister clique. She'll probably make a big deal about Brenda dating Brad, too. Pretty suspicious, huh, the stepsister of the next president going with the current president? Obviously a conspiracy, right?"

He and Ted laughed, but Janie was silent and troubled. Before she became accepted into the group, she, too, had seen it as a closed and snobby clique that ran things at Kennedy. Janie had dealt with it by becoming shy and withdrawn. Maybe Laurie's act was a different version of the same condition; maybe she deserved a chance. Then Janie looked at her friends around the table. Laurie had managed to hurt every one of them somehow. It was too late to give Laurie Bennington the benefit of the doubt.

Chapter
11

Gloria was late. Laurie sat on a stone bench in the quad, stabbing at the cover of her notebook with her pen. She knew her white jeans were probably getting filthy, but she didn't care. She could always change after gym if she needed to, and she would be going home not long after that anyway.

Where was Gloria? They had arranged by phone the night before to meet and take the nominating petitions in together, then have a strategy session. They certainly needed one. Most of Laurie's assumptions when she decided to run were turning out to be false. Dick Westergard was very far from being the nerd she had imagined, although she hadn't been so naive that she let him change her plans. She was still sure that she could win. But she wasn't going to walk away with the race the way she had expected.

More alarming, the people she had thought she

could count on were not coming through for her. A few had promised to support her, but with so little enthusiasm that she was sure they would forget about it as soon as she was out of sight. Others, like Sasha and Peter, had found reasons to stay neutral. And some had as much as said they opposed her. Even a Miss No-Personality like Janie Barstow had the guts to say that because she supported Chris for president, she wouldn't vote for Laurie for vice-president.

That was the real issue, of course. Chris and Brenda had put out the word to stop Laurie from winning — that was the unspoken reason for Peter's and Sasha's phony neutrality. The establishment at Kennedy High, the kids who thought of themselves as the only ones who really counted, had decided she was a threat to them and their power. Like the pioneers when they came under attack, they were drawing their wagons into a circle, and she was definitely on the outside, with the Indians.

So was John Marquette. Chris's crowd loved to make jokes about John because he was very big, not very bright, and had real caveman ideas about how to act with girls. On the other hand, Laurie had always gotten along pretty well with him. She enjoyed half of his remarks, pretended not to hear the others, and never got within reach when they were alone. Not only that, lots of kids at Kennedy looked up to him. He was, after all, a champion athlete who cared about the school's reputation. It wouldn't be such a terrible thing if he became president. So what if he was a few bricks shy of a load? There were plenty of politicians with no more brains than he had!

"Hi," Gloria said from behind her. "Sorry if I'm late. I was talking to a couple of people about the campaign. How has it been going?"

"Rotten," Laurie replied. She described her encounter in the lunchroom. "I think we have to write off that whole crowd," she concluded. "It just goes to show you. I thought some of them were my friends. They've been to my parties. We've spent time together. But I guess what it comes down to is that they were only using me."

"How awful," Gloria said. "Still, never mind. They think they're big shots, but their votes don't count for any more than anybody else's. All we have to do is reach the ordinary students and convince them to vote for you."

"That reminds me," Laurie said. "You know that John Marquette is running for president against Chris Austin?"

Gloria nodded.

"I think we ought to have a talk with him," Laurie continued. "See if we can agree on some sort of joint slate. Nobody in Austin's bunch is going to support me anyway, from what I've seen today, so a ticket with John can't cost us anything."

"Fantastic," said Gloria. "He'll swing the jock vote to us, and we can help him get support from all the kids who want to see a change in the way things are run around here. Do you think he'll agree, though?"

Laurie shrugged. "I don't see why not. It's as good for him as for us. Come on," she added, standing up, "let's go over to the SG office and turn the petitions in."

"Let's not forget," Gloria said as they walked down the hall, "that our most important job is beating Westergard. It's not going to be easy. His people are already starting to muddy the water."

"What does that mean?" Laurie asked sharply. She stopped and faced Gloria.

"Well. . . ." She seemed reluctant to continue.

"Come on," Laurie insisted. "What are they saying?"

"Nothing really, just childish stuff."

"For instance?"

Gloria looked away in embarrassment. "Oh, I overheard one guy make a joke about how you and John both had all your qualifications from the neck down. And his friend said, 'Yeah, and they show them off whenever they can, too.' It didn't mean anything."

Laurie's cheeks reddened. She shifted uncomfortably, suddenly aware of the draft in the hallway on her bare arms. Maybe she should have worn a blouse under the sweater today. She had tried it that way before leaving home, but this looked better. Anyway, it wasn't a crime to have a nice figure and to be proud of it. Her outfits might not fit in with what the preppy crowd was used to, but in California some people might consider her a conservative dresser. And it was straight out of the nineteen-fifties to think that brains and beauty didn't mix. She had a solid B+ average without working any more than she wanted to. Not many of *them* could say that.

"Why do you say they were Westergard's people?" she asked.

"I sort of know the first guy, and he's a chess bug. It figures he'd be a friend of Westergard."

"Hmm. . . ." Laurie couldn't believe for a moment that the sweet, sensitive boy she had been with on Friday evening was deliberately spreading nasty jokes about her. It simply didn't fit. On the other hand, he might not be able to control what his friends did. She couldn't blame him for that. "Oh well," she said. "I guess a joke or two won't hurt me."

"Not if we start some of our own going around," Gloria said eagerly. "If we can get people to think of Westergard as ridiculous, they'll support you instead. Or if we can dig up some scandal. I've already started asking around, trying to see if there's anything shady about him that we can use. There *was* some kind of stir about the budget of the chess team last fall, but I can't find anyone who remembers the details. I'll keep looking."

Laurie frowned. "If it wasn't important enough for anyone to remember, why should we bother digging it up?"

"It doesn't have to be important, as long as we can use it to plant questions about him in people's minds. The voters won't remember the details either, but they *will* remember that he was involved in some kind of financial scandal."

"Or that somebody claimed that somebody on the chess team was," Laurie said.

Gloria missed her ironic tone. "Sure. He's the

captain, isn't he? Everybody will figure that it's his responsibility."

Laurie considered arguing the point further, or ordering Gloria to drop her investigation, but she didn't know how the younger girl would react. She seemed very determined and very certain of what she was doing. If Laurie interfered too much, Gloria might lose her enthusiasm for the job. She might even quit, and Laurie couldn't afford that. It would mean the end of her campaign. She would be publicly humiliated. She could imagine what Chris and Brenda, and all their friends would say, not to mention Lars. He would go home convinced that he had been completely justified in turning his back on such a flake.

"Come on," Gloria added impatiently. "If we miss the filing deadline, we've already lost the election."

Elissa Bloom, the outgoing SG secretary, was short and plump, with cheeks that looked as if she kept crab apples stuffed in them. She looked up as they entered the office. "More customers?" she said jovially. "It's too bad we don't charge a filing fee; we might make enough to buy a new box of manila folders, and a ream or two of paper for the copying machine. What do we have here?" she added, as she took the petitions. "You're Laurie, aren't you? I thought so. I remember noticing you in the fashion show. And you're a candidate for vice-president? Um-hum." She scanned the signatures, then counted them. "Okay, that seems all in order. Good luck."

She turned to Gloria. "And what can I do for you?"

"I'm with Laurie," Gloria explained. "I'm managing her campaign."

"Oh. I thought you might be running for vice-president, too." She laughed. "I can't imagine what makes the job so popular this year. As far as I recall, Stu Grinnell, who is vice-president now, ran unopposed."

Laurie blinked. "Are there a lot of us running for vice-president?" she asked.

"No, I don't suppose so," Elissa said, "not really. There are only three so far, but that certainly *seems* like a lot, doesn't it?"

"It certainly does," Laurie said grimly. "Who are they?"

Elissa picked up a file folder and thumbed through it. "Well, there's you, of course. And a guy named Richard Westergard; you just missed him."

"Good," Gloria said under her breath.

"And the third candidate is Farley Templar."

Laurie's eyebrows knit together. "Farley Templar?" she repeated. "Who's he? I feel like I know the name. I wonder if we were in a class together last year."

"He's very active on the yearbook," Elissa said. "On the business side, I think."

"Hmph. What does he look like?"

"Pretty ordinary. About five-ten, short dark hair, dresses neatly."

Laurie's face relaxed and she shook her head. "Nope, I must have been thinking of somebody else. So he's running for vice-president, too."

"Um-hum. It should be an interesting race. Good luck," she repeated, then turned to say hello to a scared-looking freshman who wanted to run for student council.

Outside the door, Laurie turned to Gloria. "Who's Farley Templar?" she demanded. "Didn't you hear anything about him running?"

"There *was* a rumor," Gloria admitted, "but I didn't think it was worth bothering you with. Farley's no threat."

" 'Farley'? Is he a friend of yours?"

"I know him, sure. I helped sell ads for the yearbook last fall. He was the assistant business manager. I guess he's business manager now."

"Really? Does that mean he's a good salesman? There's not much difference between a salesman and a politician."

"He knows a lot about business, but I don't know how good a salesman he is. He used to brag about all the college-level business and accounting courses he was taking at night."

"I wonder why he isn't running for treasurer, then."

Gloria took her arm and led her toward the quad. "Because if he did, he'd probably win," she said. "Do you really think anybody as busy as he is wants to waste his time dealing with student government? Not a chance! If you ask me, I think he nominated himself because he figures it will look good on his college applications. It'll show that he's something more than a grind."

"Maybe so," Laurie said. "But I wish he'd gone out for Glee Club instead."

"Then he'd have to go to rehearsals. This way

111

he gets the credit, and he doesn't have to waste any of his time on it."

"Do people really think that way?" Laurie marveled. "Maybe Elissa was right, and there *should* be a filing fee — to keep out candidates like him who aren't serious. It's not fair that I should have to worry about him as well as Dick."

"*Don't* worry about him," Gloria said. "Westergard is the one we have to beat. I'd be surprised if Farley Templar even runs an active campaign. Speaking of which, we'd better make some plans, or we won't have an active campaign either."

They returned to the bench in the quad and sat down. Gloria had pages of lists and questions in her notebook, which they discussed one by one. She had already signed up a room for the volunteers' meeting, and gotten out a leaflet announcing it. Laurie in turn reported that she had asked a sophomore who did airbrush paintings on denim jackets to do a T-shirt design for her; if she got it to the silk-screen shop in the afternoon, they would deliver the shirts by Wednesday.

She took a folder of photographs for the poster from her bookbag and showed them to Gloria. Her personal favorite showed only her head and bare shoulders; the expression on her face was both sultry and somewhat mocking. Laurie's dad kept a copy of it in a silver frame on his office desk.

Gloria turned thumbs down. It might do if she was running for school mascot, she said. But it wasn't the right image for a vice-president. She flipped through the stack of pictures, and stopped at the one Laurie had been afraid she would choose. It showed Laurie in a plain white blouse, sitting next to a shining antique table. She was looking straight at the camera with a face that reminded her of a loan officer in a bank.

"I hate that," Laurie said. "I look awful."

"Wrong. You look serious. Somebody who is running for office is *supposed* to look serious."

Laurie looked doubtful.

"Trust me, Laurie; this is your campaign image. You can't let the student body think you're an airhead, or a bunny, or they won't vote for you. So how about it? Do we take this to the printer?"

"I guess so," Laurie sighed. "Golly, look at the time! I'm already late for gym."

"Cut," Gloria suggested.

Laurie laughed. "And get a reputation as a goof-off? No way — if I'm going to do this thing, I might as well do it right!"

Chapter
12

"You don't understand," Phoebe wailed, "I've just *got* to go!"

"We know how much you'd like to, dear," her mother said calmly. "And we've given it a lot of thought, but I'm afraid the answer is no."

"But Griff is counting on me to be there! I practically promised!"

"I'm sorry. You shouldn't have made a promise before speaking to us. If he stays in acting school, there will be plenty more opportunities for you to see him perform."

"*If?* Of course he'll stay in acting school, it's his whole life. Unless he's so discouraged by me not being there, that he does badly and drops out. Do you realize that you could be ruining his entire career?"

She sprang up and began to pace around the dinner table. "Why can't you let me go? I promise I won't get behind on my schoolwork. I'll even do it ahead of time and show it to you. Please?"

"That's an attractive offer," her mom said gravely, "but the answer is still no. Be sensible, Phoebe. Your father and I hardly know your friend Griffin. As for the girl who offered to let you stay with her, you don't even know her name and address, much less anything about her. I'm sure if she's a friend of your friend, she's a perfectly nice person. But who knows what kind of area she lives in? Even if she finds it safe, you're not familiar with New York City. You might easily get into difficulties."

"How am I supposed to get familiar with New York, by staying home and watching *Sesame Street*?"

"Don't be sarcastic, dear. It's very unattractive. I know how much our decision upsets you, but we are trying to look out for your best interests. You're too young to take an excursion like this all alone."

"Too young? Lots of girls my age get married!"

"And it's very foolish of them, too. Does their foolishness mean that you have to be foolish as well?"

Phoebe came to a halt in front of her mother and put her fists on her hips. "Admit it," she cried. "The truth is, you and Daddy don't trust me!"

"That's partly true," her mother said evenly. "We trust your intentions, but we don't entirely trust your ability to carry them out. We trust your good sense, but not your experience of the world beyond Rose Hill, which is very limited."

"Isn't there *anything* I can do to change your minds?"

She shook her head sadly. "No, dear, I'm afraid that's our final decision. You must simply accept the fact that you are not going to New York for your friend's play."

Phoebe stared at her silently for a long moment. "Then I won't be responsible for what happens," she said, and stalked out of the house.

As Phoebe turned onto Rossmore Road, a light drizzle began to fall from the gray evening sky. She turned up the collar of her jacket, but made no move to protect her thick, red hair. What did it matter anyway? Hands in her pockets and shoulders hunched up, she walked along, mentally replaying the conversation with her mom; trying out all the things she could have said, but didn't think of in time.

It was no use. Her parents didn't approve of Griffin and never had. If they could, they would end her relationship with him. They distrusted a boy who would drop out of high school in his senior year to go off to New York to be an actor. When she tried to tell them how talented and dedicated he was, they refused to listen. They thought he was flightly, and unstable.

She never should have told them anything about him. She should have known that they wouldn't understand. In a moment of misery, during the long months when she didn't know what had become of him, she had confided in her mother. Now her confidences were being used against her. She understood why Griffin had done what he did, but her mother refused even to try.

In her eyes, his actions proved that he was inconsiderate, immature, and unworthy of Phoebe's affection.

Phoebe couldn't let Griffin down, not when he already had suffered such terrible disappointments. He was depending on her. When he saw her in the audience opening night, her presence would inspire him to give a performance so stunning that the agents and producers would line up afterwards to offer him parts. A famous Broadway director would take the two of them for a late supper on the terrace of a rooftop restaurant, and buy champagne to toast his latest discovery. Griffin would literally have New York at his feet.

The story might have a completely different ending if he didn't find her in the audience.

She saw him pacing up and down in the wings, peeking through the curtain time after time, growing more and more nervous as his entrance drew closer, and she was still not there. He would forget his lines, dry up, ruin the play. Perhaps he would simply refuse to go on. When the curtain fell, his teachers and fellow students would not speak to him, or recognize his existence. Shamed beyond endurance, positive that he was destined to fail, he would drop out of acting school and disappear. Maybe he would join the Foreign Legion, or become a drifter. The theater would lose a great talent, and Phoebe would never see him again!

Phoebe suddenly realized that she was shivering. She blinked the rain out of her eyes and looked around. In her misery she had walked all the way to the shopping center. Right across the road, the bright window of the sub shop called to her, promising dryness and warmth, and a place to sit down for a few minutes. She hesitated, wondering if she felt ready to face anyone she knew. But then she reflected that no one hung out there at this time of day. She would be surprised if there were any other customers at all.

She *was* surprised. When she pushed open the door, she saw Ted sitting alone at the gang's usual table in the corner. He looked up and his face brightened. "Hey, Pheeb," he called. "Are you having a sub for supper, too?" He waved the remaining half of his sandwich.

"Not me," she said with a shudder. "What I need is a cup of tea."

"You're all wet." He fumbled around in his knapsack and pulled out a sweat shirt. "Here, take that jacket off and put this on. I'll get your tea. Regular or herb?"

Phoebe gave him a wan smile. Sasha had talked the owners of the sub shop into carrying a selection of herb teas, but as far as Phoebe could tell, Sasha was the only one who ever ordered any of them. "Regular, please. With milk and sugar."

The sweat shirt was comforting. By the time Ted returned with her tea, she had recovered enough to wonder what he was doing there at such an odd hour. When she asked, he made a sour face and said, "Hanging out, that's all."

"Now? Alone?"

"Yeah. Well, Woody said he might drop by."

"Where's Chris?" Even as she asked the question, she thought she knew the answer.

"Out campaigning. She and Kim have a meeting this evening with the officers of the different foreign language clubs. They're hoping for endorsements in French, German, Spanish, Italian, and Japanese."

"What happened to Greek and Latin?"

He grunted. "That's the Classics Club. They endorsed Chris this afternoon."

"She's really working at this, isn't she? Why hasn't she asked me to help? Or you?"

"Oh, she's asked me. She wanted me to call a meeting of the football team to vote on an endorsement."

"Really? I didn't know the football team went around endorsing candidates for student government."

"Neither did I. But she didn't like it much when I told her that. It's just as well for her, though. If there was a vote among the team members, it wouldn't surprise me if she lost. John's a member of the team, after all, even if he isn't the most popular guy around. I might even vote for him myself."

"Ted! What are you talking about? You'd never vote against Chris."

He refused to meet her eye. "Not really," he said in a low voice. "I couldn't bring myself to do that, I guess. But I sure won't be all broken up if she loses. This campaign is changing her, and I don't much care for the changes."

"She's been very busy, I know," Phoebe said sympathetically. "And she hasn't had as much time for you as you'd both like, but — "

"It isn't that," he said, interrupting. "Or maybe

it is, partly. What really gripes me, though, is this new attitude she's getting. I think she's trying to be the kind of person she thinks a politician is supposed to be."

"Oh, Ted. I'm sure you're — "

He overrode her. "Do you want to know what she did when I told her I didn't want to poll the football team? Right in front of Kim she accused me of being afraid of John Marquette! There's no one on earth but her I'd take that from, and I don't like taking it from her."

Phoebe was shocked. Ted Mason was one of the most easy-going guys she knew. Even when he was quarterbacking an important game, he had a sort of loose-limbed, take-it-as-it-comes grace that suggested he might curl up for a nap at any moment. Now, however, he was sitting hunched over, fists clenched, as wound up as a spring.

The idea that Ted was afraid of John Marquette was laughable; he was no coward. Only weeks before, he had faced Marquette and ordered him to leave his party after Marquette picked a fight with Sasha's new boyfriend. Marquette was spoiling for a fight, but he took a good look at Ted and left shortly after that.

No, Phoebe thought, the real problem was Chris. She was terribly conscientious and strict with herself, but she kept trying to force that on other people as well. She refused to make allowances for their different characters and attitudes. Worse still, once she made up her mind about the right thing to do, she forgot that others might honestly disagree.

"Ted, that's awful," Phoebe said. "But you

know she didn't mean it. The pressures of the campaign are getting to her a little, that's all. After next week she'll be her old self again, you'll see."

"I doubt it," he said glumly. "Either she wins, which makes her sure that she's been right about everything all along. Or she loses and goes around blaming herself and everyone else for not working hard enough. I'm starting to wish I'd agreed to run instead of her. I would have known enough not to take the whole business too seriously."

Phoebe wanted to argue, but she had to agree with him. Rather than say so and add fuel to the fire, she silently sipped her tea and studied the faded color poster for hot veal parmigiana submarine sandwiches that hung on the wall just over Ted's head. The sub in the picture really looked like a piece of rye bread with pink icing on top. Even so, her stomach growled. Her mother had probably left some supper on the stove for her.

"Hey," Ted said, "what's doing with you? How come you're walking around in the rain?"

"I just had to get out of the house — a fight with my mom."

"That's tough. I thought you and your folks got along pretty well."

"We do, usually," she admitted. "But not this time." She told him about Griffin's invitation and her parents' flat refusal to let her go to New York.

"What a shame," he said. "You must feel bummed out about missing something like that. I remember that number you and Griffin did in the Follies last fall. You were great together."

"Thanks," Phoebe said darkly. "But I'm not

sure I *am* going to miss his show, I'm not sure at all."

Ted gave her an odd look, but didn't say anything. After draining his soda, he glanced at his watch. "I'd better get going, I've got a quiz in trig tomorrow. Do you want a ride home?"

"Sure, thanks. And I'm going to have a talk with Chris. Someone has to make her see what the campaign is doing to her, and to you, too."

"Good luck," he replied. "But if you want to talk to Chris, don't be surprised if you have to ask Kim for an appointment. The campaign comes first."

Once home, Phoebe managed to gulp down some warmed-over pot roast, potatoes, and salad without having to speak to her parents. As she went up the stairs, she could hear them in the living room, laughing with Shawn over something on TV. A feeling of sadness came over her, and a hopeless wish that she could be ten years old again and sit between Mommy and Daddy laughing at the TV, instead of creeping off to her room to plot a rebellion.

She tried to call Chris, but Mrs. Austin said that she and Kim were still at a meeting. Phoebe felt some of the frustration Ted had expressed. Chris used to be there when she wanted to talk with her. All this political stuff had become more important to her than her old friend. Phoebe knew that this reaction was terribly unfair, but knowing that didn't make it go away.

At least Sasha was still at the bookshop. Phoebe quickly filled her in on the crisis with her parents over the trip to New York. "I don't know what to do," she concluded. "I really don't."

"What can you do?" Sasha replied. "You'll have to tell Griffin that you can't come this time, that's all. It's tough, but that's the way it is."

Phoebe was taken aback by her response. Sasha was usually the dreamiest, most romantic, of their crowd. She had fallen in love at first sight with Wes. Phoebe had been sure that she would advise her to go to Griffin's show, whatever the consequences.

She tried again. "Sash, I can't do that to him. I'll *die* if I don't get up there. I'd be letting him down so badly."

"Hasn't he ever let you down badly?"

"That's different. He felt he had to do what he did."

"Uh-huh. And you have to stay in Rose Hill instead of going to New York."

"Well, I don't *really* have to, do I? If I took a plane, I could leave after lunch on Saturday, see the show, spend some time with Griffin, and still be back the next morning. If I had a friend to cover for me, just for that one night, it would work out just fine — wouldn't it?"

"Phoebe," Sasha said warningly, "if you mean me, the answer's no. After all the lies we told when Wes and I went up to your dad's cabin, I'm all lied out. Besides, my parents asked me to promise not to deceive them that way again, and I have to keep my promise. If you listen to me, you'll do the same. You might feel bad about missing Griffin's show, but you'll feel a lot worse if you tell your parents a lot of lies. Especially when they find out."

"Why should they find out? It's just one evening!"

"Oh, come on," Sasha said, "you've got a brain between your ears, Phoebe! What are they going to think when you announce that you're staying over at a friend's house, on the same night that you've begged to go to New York? Don't you think they'll call your friend and ask to speak to you? What then?"

"You could say I'm in the bathroom and I'll call back. Then you call the theater and leave a message for me, and I could call them back."

"Phoebe, A: It'll never work, it's too complicated. Something is bound to get messed up. B: It's dishonest and wrong, and you shouldn't do it. And C: If you insist on going ahead with this crazy idea, you'll have to find yourself a different accomplice. I just can't."

The frustration that had been accumulating all evening boiled over. "Sasha Jenkins," she said in an icy voice, "I thought I could count on you. I thought we were friends. And I hope you need help someday and come begging to me, so that I can remind you what kind of help you gave me when I needed it."

"You don't mean that," Sasha cried. Phoebe took some satisfaction from the anguish in her voice. "You're just feeling bad because of everything that's happened, and you're taking it out on me."

Phoebe knew Sasha was telling the truth. "Oh, I'm sorry, Sash," she said, her voice trembling.

"I just want this so badly I'm willing to try anything."

"It's okay, Phoebe. You know I'd help if I could. Maybe you'll find a way."

"I hope so." Phoebe hung up the phone, then stared at her own face in the mirror. Her nose was still burned from her work in the garden, her eyes puffy with fatigue, and sadness. After a few moments, her lower lip began to tremble and her throat moved convulsively. With an abrupt movement, she flung herself on the bed and buried her face in her pillow as her shoulders began to shake.

Chapter
13

Chris stepped back and examined her image in the full-length mirror on the back of her door. Since the campaign began, she was giving more time than usual to deciding what to wear. This morning she had tried on two other possibilities before choosing a blue and white Oxford-cloth shirt, a miniskirt, and vest of light, blue cotton.

After a close scrutiny, she decided that the outfit was just right. With her blond hair and classic features, it made her look like a modern young executive. The button-down shirt gave a feeling of crisp efficiency, and the skirt and vest said that she wasn't old-fashioned, or stuffy. All she needed now was a touch of flair.

She was trying on a twisted necklace of blue, amber, and clear beads when the telephone rang in the hall. A moment later, her stepsister Brenda called, "Chris, it's for you. It's Sasha."

"Thanks," Chris said, and took the phone. "Hi, Sash. What's up?"

"I wanted to tell you yesterday, but I didn't think I ought to. When you get to school this morning, take a look at *The Red and the Gold*. There's a front-page editorial endorsing you for president."

"Sasha, how great! Oh, I can't wait to see it!"

"I ought to warn you that it's pretty positive about John, too. The members of the editorial board were impressed by some of his ideas."

"Ideas?" Chris said. "John Marquette hasn't had an idea in the last five years!"

After a noticeable silence, Sasha asked, "Did Brad speak to you yet about having a candidates' forum next Tuesday, after school?"

"Uh-huh, I ran into him yesterday afternoon. I told him I'm all for it. But do you think students will hang around to listen to a lot of speeches?"

"Oh, I think so. The election is stirring up a lot of feeling, you know. I'd better run; Woody is picking me up this morning."

Chris replaced the receiver, and stared unseeing at the little watercolor of Venice that hung over the telephone table. She felt good about the endorsement; but it had never really crossed her mind that the paper *wouldn't* endorse her. They couldn't have seriously considered recommending John Marquette for president. It was hard to imagine, but that was what Sasha had hinted. And if they, among the most sophisticated people at Kennedy, claimed to be impressed by his platform, he could certainly fool the average student.

It suddenly occurred to Chris that she might actually lose the race. Her stomach lurched as if the room had suddenly become a swiftly descending elevator. There was no way she ought to lose. She had done everything just as she was supposed to. She had the support of almost every academic club, and the endorsement of the school paper. It was too bad that some people — some people named Ted — were unwilling to do their part and build support among athletes. But with that exception, she thought she had covered every important group of students.

She hadn't considered the possibility her campaign might fail; but she couldn't pretend to believe that the best candidate *always* won. To be rejected in favor of somebody like John Marquette would totally humiliate her. She just wouldn't allow it to happen. Between this morning and Wednesday she was going to devote every moment, every bit of energy she had, to campaigning. She had been hoping to take some time off over the weekend, to spend a few hours alone with Ted, but that was impossible. She couldn't afford it. She was so preoccupied with thoughts of the election that she wouldn't be very good company for him anyway.

"Chris?" Brenda called. "Are you ready? Dad's in a hurry."

"Coming," she called back. She stepped inside the door of her room for a quick look around, then went downstairs to the car.

The first thing Chris saw when she got to school was a hand-lettered poster that said: WESTERGARD FOR VEEP. Someone had spent a lot of time and

effort drawing a picture of Kennedy High with a
field of totally imaginary flowers in front of it.
Someone else had torn it down and ripped it into
four pieces. Across one piece was scrawled in
red, *B.E.S.T.* It took her a moment to realize that
these were the initials of the Beat the Establishment System Together John and Laurie had organized.

Her own poster, designed by Kim, was quiet
and dignified. Over her picture from last year's
yearbook, it said: LET'S KEEP KENNEDY MOVING,
and under the picture: CHRIS AUSTIN FOR PRESI-
DENT. Kim had had a hundred of them printed
at the copy shop, and put them all over school.
This morning Chris could not find one of them
still up. Someone, or some group, had made a
clean sweep. She did not think it would be very
hard to figure out who.

Apparently the vandalism had angered others
as much as it did her. Laurie's posters were still
on the bulletin boards and lampposts, but most
of them had been defaced with inked-in beards,
moustaches, and obscene suggestions. Chris
didn't approve of retaliation, but was grimly
pleased to see it just the same.

The nearest bins of *The Red and the Gold*
were near the front entrance. She stalked across
the quadrangle. Her enemies might tear down
her posters, but they couldn't steal the endorsement of the paper from her.

When Chris got to the bins, however, she
found them empty. Puzzled, she went around to
the bins near the lunchroom, but they too were
empty. It was still early, too early for kids to

have grabbed every last copy; maybe the delivery van hadn't arrived yet. She started in the direction of the newspaper office, but halfway there she met Sasha. Sasha was pale and trembling.

"Hey, you look sick," Chris said with concern in her voice. "Do you need to sit down?"

"I need to scream!" Sasha replied. "How could they do that to my newspaper? It's the most disgusting thing I've ever heard of!"

"Who? What? Did the printers mess things up? Where *is* the paper, anyway? I couldn't find a copy all over school."

"Neither could I. But when I called the printers, they said that their man had put them in the bins this morning, the same as usual. That's when I smelled a rat. How could this issue, with all the election coverage and endorsements, turn up missing? It couldn't be an accident. So I started hunting around."

Chris grabbed her arm. "And what happened? Did you find the papers? Where were they?"

"In the dumpster behind the cafeteria, with a ton or so of kitchen garbage all over them. Three thousand newspapers, a total loss. It made me want to throw up. Who would do such a thing? It's like burning books! And besides, *The Red and the Gold* is *our* newspaper. It's supported and paid for by the whole school. It belongs to us. To destroy it that way is like kicking us all in the face!"

"I never thought they would sink so low," Chris said in a steely voice. "We can't let something like this go by."

"Who are you talking about?"

"Oh come on, Sash, face facts. The paper endorses me over John Marquette, and that issue gets dumped. You don't need Sherlock Holmes, do you?"

Sasha shook her head. "John isn't one of my favorite people," she said, "but I don't think he'd do such a thing. He was really looking forward to seeing his interview. Besides, if he had read the editorial he would have seen that it was pretty positive about him, even though it ended up endorsing you. It wouldn't have made sense for him to destroy it."

"I don't think he has the brains to see that. But maybe you're right. In that case there's only one answer, and it's staring us right in the face."

Sasha turned. Chris was looking fixedly at Laurie, who had just entered the quad and was about to sit down. She was wearing a bright red dress of some clingy, knit fabric that began with tank-top straps and ended in a miniskirt. Bright red jelly shoes and a gold chain anklet completed the outfit.

"Do you really believe — " Sasha began.

"You bet I do," Chris said through clenched teeth, and started across the quad. She had put up with Laurie's attempts to keep her from becoming homecoming princess the previous fall. She had even tried to excuse Laurie's slanderous gossiping about Brenda, but this was different. Sasha was right — this time Laurie had hurt every student at Kennedy High.

Laurie glanced up as she approached and blinked in alarm. When Chris stopped an arm's length away, Laurie stood up and faced her with an expression of defiance.

Chris shook off Sasha's restraining hand and said loudly, "I'm surprised you have the nerve to show your face around here." Looking her up and down, she added, "Not to mention as much else of yourself as you think you can get away with!"

"You don't own this school yet, Austin," Laurie replied, just as loudly. "And if the students have any sense, you never will. I have just as much right to be here as you do."

"After what you did, you don't deserve to have any rights at all!"

"What did I do? Dare to run for office? Dare to get together with other kids who are sick of the clique that's been running this school? Dare to support someone besides you for president? Well, let me tell you something, Little Miss Preppy. B.E.S.T. is going to sweep you and your whole crowd right onto the garbage heap where you belong!"

Several of the growing crowd of spectators cheered, and others laughed. To Chris, who heard in Laurie's final words a cynical confession of guilt, this was too much. "You won't get away with it," she screamed. "I'll see that you pay for every last paper you destroyed, and then I'll see you're expelled! There's no place at Kennedy for someone like you!"

Laurie's face turned nearly the shade of her dress. As she turned to walk away Chris reached to stop her, but somebody dragged her away by the elbows.

"You idiot," Ted's voice said in her ear. "What do you think you're doing? Do you want a suspension on your record for fighting, right before the election?"

"I don't care," she panted, "as long as Laurie gets what's coming to her!" She twisted from side to side, but Ted's grip was too firm to evade.

"What got you in such an uproar?" he asked. "I've never seen you like this."

"I've never been so mad," she declared. "Laurie destroyed the whole issue of *The Red and the Gold*, by dumping it in the garbage. She can't get away with it."

Ted whistled. "You saw her do that? That's terrible."

"I didn't see her," Chris admitted. "But I know she's responsible."

"Oh? How?"

The doubt in his voice exasperated her. "Well, *somebody* did it. Who else had a motive?"

"I don't know, but it's pretty amazing when you think about it. Let's see, each of those bundles must weight about fifty pounds, and there are ten or fifteen of them, I guess. She's pretty strong to handle so much weight, isn't she? And she did it without getting any ink on her hands or dress, too."

"Ted Mason, don't you try to confuse me! I didn't say she did it all herself, I said she was responsible. She must have had help, that's all. But she's the one in back of it. She's bound to be!"

Laurie was fuming. How *dare* Chris Austin

133

stand up in the middle of the quad and threaten her! If John and Gloria hadn't stopped her, she would have barged into the radio station to demand equal time. Laurie was the one whose posters had been ruined, after all. She had felt miserable seeing all those rude remarks and crude drawings on her picture. It was almost like being scrawled on herself.

Gloria was positive that Dick Westergard's friends had put the graffiti on her posters. Laurie wasn't so sure. All week long, Dick had been friendly to her in the halls, even if he was staging an energetic campaign. She didn't want to believe it, and now she felt she had a stronger suspect: Chris Austin. It wasn't the kind of thing she would have expected from such a prissy girl, but that was before this morning's exhibition. Anyone who was so obviously off in the twinky zone might do almost anything at all.

It was time for home room. Laurie melted into the stream of traffic going her way and let it carry her along while she brooded about Austin. When she looked up, she saw Dick Westergard coming toward her. The effect caught her by surprise. Her breath quickened, and butterflies tickled the inside of her tummy.

She smiled and opened her mouth to say hello. His expression became stony and he walked right by without looking at her. Laurie came to a dead stop in the middle of the corridor and stared after him. Maybe he hadn't noticed her. But she knew he had looked straight at her, then his expression had changed. That couldn't have been accident or coincidence. He had seen her and chosen not to acknowledge her existence. It was as if he was trying to wipe her from the face of the earth.

A young boy, probably a freshman, bumped into her, muttered an apology, and then stared at her. It was only then that Laurie felt the tears on her cheeks. She tried to tell herself that they were tears of fury, but deep inside she knew better.

As he entered home room, several of Dick's friends waved to him. He nodded back absentmindedly and took his seat. He clasped his hands on the desktop and stared down at them. His fingers, interlaced and twisting, seemed like a good model for his thoughts. Though they were all connected, they also worked against each other.

Playing with the analogy was more comfortable than allowing himself to recall Laurie's face as he passed her in the hall. He had deliberately avoided looking directly at her. But in his peripheral vision he saw first, the warm smile of greeting, then the look of disbelief, then an expression exactly like one of his sisters' in the instant between hurting herself and starting to cry. Except that Laurie hadn't hurt herself; *he* had hurt her.

Until the last week, Dick's life had been orderly and simple, like a good computer program. But ever since that afternoon at Laurie Bennington's house, he had been completely confused. From what people said, she was manipulative, selfish, and about as trustworthy as an angry scorpion. Maybe she had been pretending to be bewildered and hurt, to keep her little game with him going.

If so, she was in for a surprise. He wasn't going to forget what she had done, just because she could make her lower lip tremble when she wanted to. On election day he was going to wipe the floor with her. He was going to make sure that she, and everybody at Kennedy, understood that his was a victory for clean and decent campaigning.

Roll call began, but he continued to pursue his thoughts. There were some advantages to having a last name that started with W.

He had been aware of Laurie for several months, but only as that girl who wore the hot outfits. When he found out that she was running against him for vice-president, his response was to burst out laughing. Her looks told him she was an obvious airhead. He doubted if she had ever had a thought in her life that didn't relate to clothes, unless it was about makeup or hair. A few friends might vote for her out of loyalty, but aside from them, he had the election in the bag.

Then he had met her, and all his preconceived ideas evaporated. Sure, she was sexy, but that wasn't all there was to her. First of all, she was by no means dumb. She was also sweet, and thoughtful, and clever. And she was touchingly vulnerable in ways she didn't even recognize. When he had held her, he was torn between passion, and a desire to comfort and reassure her. After the evening they spent together, he had decided that once the campaign was over he wanted to see more of her.

After school on Monday he had had a strategy meeting with his friends Tom Petitt and Arnie

136

Kindred, who were acting as co-campaign managers. The meeting went smoothly, until Arnie raised the question of how to deal with the two other candidates.

"I don't think Templar is serious about running," Tom said. "A friend of his told me that he just wants to be able to say he ran when he fills out his applications for college scholarships — civic duty and all that. As for Bennington, I think we ought to needle her in little ways. Sooner or later she'll blow up and let the whole school see how nasty she is."

"What do you mean, nasty?" Dick asked casually. "I think she's very nice."

"Laurie Bennington?" Tom hooted. "She's the original Dragon Lady! How well do you know her?"

"Not very well," he admitted. "But I liked what I saw."

Arnie laughed. "If she was in one of her usual numbers, I'll bet you saw plenty, too!"

"That's not what I meant at all! Come on, Tom. Seriously, why do you talk about her that way?"

"Well, for starters, do you know a girl named Brenda Austin? She's the stepsister of Chris Austin, the one's who's running for president."

"Yeah, I guess so," Dick said with a shrug. "Didn't she write an article in the paper last fall about that halfway house in D.C.?"

"That's the one. Well, I was in history with her last term. Kind of mixed up, but really a good kid. Then Laurie Bennington made her life miserable supposedly to get back at Chris for something. She even talked about her over KND, if you can believe it. If you'd seen Brenda's face while all that was going on, you'd know why I think Laurie's a complete witch."

Dick had left the meeting unconvinced. He could easily believe that the Laurie he knew could be sharp-tongued and wounding to people she disliked. And he was prepared to admit that, like most other people, she might unthinkingly do mean and nasty things now and then. But he could not bring himself to think that Tom was right about her whole personality. The girl he had been with simply was not that kind of person.

As the week went on, he began to wonder. At first the incidents were so minor that they were laughable, but soon they started to get on his nerves. Someone chalked WIMP on his locker, then did it again each time he wiped it off. A classmate asked him if it was true that the chess team had been padding its budget, and was about to be suspended by student government. In the halls, small groups of kids, some of them wearing the new B.E.S.T. armbands, fell silent as he approached, then burst into laughter as soon as he was past.

After school on Thursday, he and his friends had put up over a dozen big, colorful posters in different areas of the school. It hadn't been easy, because he insisted that they not disturb the posters of other candidates, even if it meant passing up a prime location — that had meant Laurie's posters. Everywhere he went, her face stared from a glossy, professionally printed poster. Every classroom had one, and the bulletin board

138

opposite the doors to the lunchroom was covered with them. Arnie wanted to take down all but one on the grounds that she was hogging space that belonged to all the candidates equally, but Dick refused to let him. True, it didn't seem fair for her to use the whole board, but he didn't intend to let Laurie's unfairness lead him to be unfair as well.

When he got to school this morning, however, he discovered that every one of his posters had been torn down and ripped up. A cold fury seized him. He had tried to be fair, to give her the benefit of the doubt, and this was the result. She was everything Tom had said. She was worse; she had deliberately made a fool of him. She had played with his affection and had pretended to enjoy that evening at his house with his sisters. But the whole time she had been secretly laughing at all of them.

Anne and Melissa had already asked several times when Laurie was coming over next. As he had made his way to home room, he kept wondering. What could he tell them the next time they asked?

Then he looked up and saw Laurie coming down the hall toward him. He didn't know whether he wanted to accuse her or beg her to explain, so he took a coward's way out. He did nothing. He pretended not to see her. But he knew that she knew that he had seen her. In that way, he got vengeance for the destruction of his posters and all the other incidents without risking a scene. Put like that, it sounded pretty clever. But he felt completely miserable about it.

"Hey, Westergard," someone whispered hoarsely. "Wake up, the period's over!"

He blinked and looked around. People were collecting their books and leaving the room. The advance guard of the next class was already filtering in and taking seats. He grabbed his notebook and scrambled up, almost tripping on the leg of his chair. He walked a little faster, intending to catch up to one of his classmates. Suddenly he stopped; Laurie was standing just outside the classroom door, and she was obviously waiting for him.

He took a deep breath. He was not going to pretend not to see her, not again. But he wasn't going to get into a fight either, not if he could help it. He stepped out the door, met her eye, nodded coolly, and turned to walk in the direction of his next class.

After three steps he was sure that she had changed her mind about confronting him. He felt relieved. What was the point of two rival candidates standing in the corridor calling each other names? All it would do was create gossip that wouldn't help either of them. He released the breath he had been holding.

"That was a really rotten thing to do," a low voice said in his ear, "and I want to know why you did it."

He stopped walking and turned to face her. "I don't know what — " he began to say, but he couldn't finish the sentence.

Laurie took his silence for the admission it was. "What did I ever do to make you treat me this way?" she demanded. "Run against you? But

I didn't run against you. I didn't even know you or know you were running."

"I don't — "

She gave a bitter laugh. "I was thinking of dropping out of the race, you know that? After I met you, I didn't want to campaign against you. Now that I know what you're really like, I'm going to get a real kick out of beating you. No one who can be as mean as you were just now, deserves to be elected assistant dogcatcher. And don't think you can win by marking up my posters, either. I'll just print more of them, as many as I have to. I'm not going to be driven out of the race!"

"But I don't want to — "

He was talking to her back. As he watched her walk away, he was plunged once more into confusion. She hadn't sounded a bit like someone with a guilty conscience. Either she was a great actress or she had no conscience at all. Or he — and everybody else at Kennedy — was wrong about her. He found himself very much wanting to believe that, but he couldn't ignore all that had happened however much he wanted to. *He* was the one whose posters had been destroyed.

A few steps down the hall he passed a bulletin board. From a location in dead center, Laurie's photograph watched him. Someone had added a balloon coming from her mouth, with the words: "I'm gonna get you!"

Chapter
14

Phoebe had planned to spend Saturday morning working in the garden, but when she looked out her bedroom window she saw only overcast skies, and the start of a slow, but persistent rain. Over breakfast she began to debate straightening out her closet and dresser, and working on her paper for English. She couldn't decide which she wanted to do less. Just when she was at the point of flipping a coin, the telephone rang. She grabbed for it the way a hungry baby grabs for a bottle.

"Hi ho," Woody's voice said. "Is this weather giving you the Phoebe-jeebies?"

"Is it!"

"How would you like a drive in the country in my glamorous red sports car?"

"In the rain?" Phoebe said dubiously.

"I'll consult the weather map and drive toward the sun. We'll take along some bread and cheese, and pretend we're on our way to a polo match."

"Well. . . ."

"Say yes," he pleaded. There was an undercurrent of urgency in his voice that she didn't understand, but decided to respond to.

"Okay. I'll need twenty minutes to get ready."

"You got it, Pheeb-a-rebop."

Eighteen minutes later he was at the front door with a large yellow and green golf embrella that looked as if it might carry him out to sea on the first good gust of wind. "We have to keep your hairdo dry," he explained, comically eyeing her tangled mass of red curls.

He insisted on keeping a stately distance behind her on the way to the curb, even though it meant that neither of them had the umbrella's full protection. Phoebe giggled at his absurd antics, sweeping the door of the Volvo open with a courtly bow that nearly poked the umbrella in her face, but she was also just a little bit concerned. For years Woody had had a huge, hopeless crush on her that faded out when he and Kim fell in love. Phoebe cherished him as a dear, close friend, but she hated it when he got all gooey. This morning's behavior was not quite gooey, but she sensed a slightly sticky surface on it.

She enjoyed sitting back and letting someone else drive, without worrying about where they were going. Woody's newest purchase was an inexpensive tape deck, and he allowed her to choose the cassettes. She selected a mellow, new wave party tape of Woody's favorite female groups singing their hits.

Some time later she blinked and looked around.

They were on a narrow road with woods on the right and a sloping meadow to the left. In the distance, under a clump of trees, were half a dozen cattle. "Where are we?" she asked.

"Somewhere in Virginia," Woody replied. "They say it's better in the South, and I thought maybe the 'it' referred to the weather."

"You were misinformed," she said dryly, looking at the rain.

He caught the reference to a favorite line from the movie *Casablanca* and laughed.

"Where's Kim today?" she asked, then quickly added, "I know, working on the campaign."

"Give the little lady sixty-four dollars! Yeah," he continued in his normal voice. "She and Chris are planning their tactics for the big debate next week. Chris stands there and tries to answer all the hard questions Kim throws at her."

Phoebe was startled. "I didn't know there were going to be questions allowed at the candidates' forum. I'd heard that everyone running was going to make a presentation and that was it."

"As far as I know, you're absolutely right."

"But why — "

"Suppose they change the format? Chris has to be prepared with responses to anything anyone might ask her. They've put together a briefing book that must be two inches thick."

"That's crazy!"

"I know," he sighed. "But I'm glad to find out that you think so, too. Whenever I try to say a word, Kim says I'm a latent male chauvinist who believes deep down that women aren't equipped to hold public office."

"That's ridiculous!"

"I know," he repeated. "But if I try to argue, it just proves what she said, or so she claims. So I keep my mouth shut and stay out of their way."

"Oh, Woody," she said sympathetically. "It must be awful for you."

He grinned. "Awful to keep my mouth shut, you mean? No, seriously, I'm not enjoying it. You know what Kim is usually like, so perky and quirky, and full of fun. Well, now it's as if she's signed up for a crusade. She's totally lost her sense of humor."

"Hmm. I guess she's afraid that Marquette might be elected president if she doesn't do everything she can to stop him."

"True, but I've had my run-ins with John, as you know, and I'm not so sure he'd be a total disaster. I read Sasha's interview with him in *The Red and the Gold*."

"How?" Phoebe said in surprise.

"Climbed into the dumpster, and fished out a copy," he replied proudly. "I figured if someone went to so much trouble to keep me from reading it, it must be worth reading. Anyway, Marquette has some pretty good ideas about what student government can do to make Kennedy a more attractive place."

"I hope you didn't tell that to Kim or Chris."

"And find myself waving from the top of the school flagpole, right below Old Glory? No thanks!" The car began to slow down. "That sign said there's a roadside park just ahead. How about some bread and cheese? The best I could do in twenty minutes was a loaf of French and some

145

sliced Wisconsin Swiss," he added anxiously as he turned off the road.

"Oh, Woody." She laughed. "You can always cheer me up, no matter how black things seem!"

"Now hold on, the object of this trip was for *you* to cheer *me* up. Let's just keep our eyes on the ball here," he said in a stern voice, then added, "Do things seem black, Pheeb?"

"I'm afraid so," she sighed. "Sasha's right, I can't lie to them after everything that's happened. But I can't let Griffin down."

"What will you do?" he asked sympathetically, handing her a dry Swiss cheese sandwich.

"The only thing I can think of is tell them straight out that I'm going, with or without their permission. What are they going to do, lock me in my room and feed me soup through the keyhole?"

"Whatever they do, it won't be much fun for any of you. Don't you think Griffin would understand if you told him — "

"*No!* I won't tell him! He needs me there, Woody. I know he does. I can't distract him with my problems at a time like this, when he needs all his concentration."

"There'll be other showcases."

"How do I know there will? If he does badly, he might be so discouraged that he quits acting school."

"You still have a couple of weeks, don't you?" he said. "Let it ride, don't do anything you can't undo. Anything might happen between now and then."

"Sure," she said gloomily. "I could be hit by a bus."

"Or Griffin could get a real part and drop out of the showcase. Let it ride, Pheebarooni; you're worrying yourself sick."

"I guess you're right."

"By the way, do you want that sandwich?"

She glanced at the intact bread and cheese in her left hand and laughed. "No, I guess not. What about the polo match?"

"Will you accept noontime traffic on the Beltway as a substitute?"

"Good show, chap," she said, as he put the car in gear and started home.

By the time they got back to Phoebe's house, the rain had stopped and the clouds were beginning to break. They found Ted in the driveway shooting baskets with Phoebe's younger brother Shawn, and trying to explain the difference between zone defense and one-on-one. He waved, pulled on his T-shirt, and joined them in the front yard.

"Hey, Woody," he said. "Give me five."

"Ted, my man," Woody said with a grin, setting out on a complicated series of hand gyrations that ended with them interlocking bent right arms and each holding his own left earlobe.

Phoebe cracked up. "Have you been rehearsing all week?" she demanded. "Or are you both members of the same lodge?"

"It's something to do." Ted shrugged. "Did you talk to Chris yet?"

She shook her head. "She's been too busy, and I've had other things on my mind."

147

"I guess you heard what happened yesterday between her and Laurie."

"I got a word-for-word account. Look, Ted, Chris is under a lot of pressure. It has to show up somewhere."

"*I* know that, but she doesn't. She thinks she's acting just the way she always does."

"That's not good. Can't Brenda talk to her?"

Ted shook his head. "Whether she can or not, she won't. I don't blame her; after all that time that she and Chris weren't getting along, she doesn't want to risk the relationship."

"Are you trying to tell me that her friends are too afraid of Chris to tell her the truth?"

"Yes," he said quietly, "that's exactly right. Either they're too afraid, or she won't listen when they try. You've got to do something, Phoebe. You're her best friend, she'll *have* to listen to you."

"All right, I'll try. Do you know if she's home?"

"She was an hour ago." He gave Woody a toss of his head. "I think Kim's looking for you. You might try the sub shop."

"Really? Thanks, Ted." He started for his car, then paused. "Pheeb, do you want a lift?"

"No, go ahead," she replied. "I'll ride my bike over to Chris's."

"Hello, Phoebe," Mrs. Austin said. "Chris is in the breakfast room. Why don't you find your own way back?"

Phoebe stopped near the archway that divided the breakfast room from the kitchen. Her friend was sitting at the table, engrossed in a big loose-leaf notebook. Blue smudges under her eyes revealed how tired she was.

Phoebe moved slightly, and Chris looked up. A smile lit up her face, then vanished so quickly, Phoebe was not certain she had seen it. "Hello," she said in a withdrawn voice.

"Hi, Chris. How are you?"

"Busy," was the reply. "Busy, and tired. Is Ted with you?"

"No," Phoebe said. The question surprised her. "He was over at our place earlier, though, shooting baskets with Shawn."

"It must be nice to have so few responsibilities — or so little awareness of the ones you do have."

"Ted is one of the most responsible people around, and you know it."

"Do I? I'm beginning to wonder. But you seem to be getting to know him much better lately."

Phoebe let that pass. "Look, Chris, I didn't come over to talk about Ted. The thing is, some of your friends are getting worried about the way things are going."

"They are? Well, it's about time! The whole future of Kennedy is at stake."

"I don't mean with the election, I mean with you."

"Me? I'm all right . . . or I will be, if some of my so-called friends would stop trying to get me to abandon what I'm doing."

"That's just the kind of thing I mean," Phoebe said. "A month ago you wouldn't have dreamed of talking about 'so-called friends.' "

"Maybe I've learned something in the last month."

"Yes, and maybe you've forgotten something, too. Remember that I was one of the people who helped convince you to run for president? I did it because I thought I could count on you to be conscientious, patient, and always fair."

"You can," Chris said.

"Can I? Is it fair to accuse a person of something, try her without giving her a chance to respond, and decide on her guilt in front of a crowd of people?"

"Bennington got to you, I see," Chris said coldly. "What did she offer, an acting job for Griffin on her father's TV station?"

Phoebe's face darkened, but she kept her voice level. "Chris, stand back and listen to yourself. You've become suspicious, and unsympathetic. That's not really you, I know it isn't. We know each other too well. You're letting this election get to you. Somehow you've *got* to walk away from it — at least stand back and take a good look."

Chris stood up. "You come here and tell me what I've *got* to do? Well, listen, Phoebe Hall. If there's any walking away to be done, why don't you start by walking away from Ted!"

"Ted's a friend of mine," Phoebe said, tossing her head. "He also happens to be in love with you, as you'd know if you took your nose out of that briefing book for five minutes."

"Do you seriously want me to go to the forum unprepared? To make a fool of myself in front of everybody? You wanted me to run, Phoebe. You said I owed it to Kennedy. Now you act as though you want me to lose the election. I can't figure out the change in you."

Phoebe stared at her silently for a long moment before saying, "If this is what the campaign has done to you, Chris, then yes, I do hope you lose the election. Not because I'm jealous of you, but because I love you and I hate what you're turning into. And I hope that sometime, maybe before you fall asleep tonight, you'll think about what I've said and what you've said. Then ask yourself which of us really has your best interests at heart."

She turned to go, then looked back with her eyes glistening. "Chris? If you ever want to talk, just call. I mean it, anytime."

Chris turned away, sat down at the table, and picked up the briefing book. Phoebe waited a moment, then walked away. At the front door she looked back. Chris was still sitting in the same position, motionless and silent.

Chapter
15

Personality conflicts and petty squabbles have no
place in Student Government! If you want an efficient, businesslike, and DIGNIFIED administration,
Vote for
FARLEY TEMPLAR
for Vice-President

Laurie made a disgusted noise, crumpled up
the leaflet, and threw it at the wastebasket. It hit
the rim and bounced onto the floor. She decided
to let it lie there.

Everyone at Kennedy would understand that
Templar's leaflet was a dig at her. Chris's yelling
match with her in the quad on Friday had been
the talk of the school. Since then, the incidents
had continued and even escalated. This morning
she had come upon three guys wearing B.E.S.T.
armbands encircling and threatening a kid who
was trying to leaflet for Dick. When she told them

to stop it and go away, they claimed that one of Dick's people, who were now calling themselves the Westerguards, had stolen and destroyed *their* supply of leaflets. If they were being kept from getting the truth to the students, they demanded, why should they permit the Westerguards to go on spreading their lies?

There was worse to come. During lunch, John had walked over to the table where Dick was eating and announced loudly that if Dick's supporters didn't stop tearing down B.E.S.T.'s posters, he was personally going to tie Westergard into a pretzel. When ten or twelve Westerguards came to Dick's side, a like number of armband-wearing B.E.S.T. members lined up behind John. Remarks and insults started to fly back and forth. Just as someone threw a roll, the teachers on duty hurried over and separated the two sides. They prevented a pitched battle, but they couldn't do anything about the angry feelings that had been stirred up. In the course of the afternoon Laurie heard of several name-calling incidents, and at least one fight in the halls.

She was also concerned to see that while her supporters and Dick's were keeping each other busy, a crew working for Farley Templar was blanketing the school with leaflets like the one she had just thrown away. They were getting a good response, too. Laurie overheard several students deploring the bitterness of the campaign and voicing support for Templar as the rational alternative. She wanted to reply, to put out a leaflet attacking Templar's idea of treating student government as a business instead of a public service.

153

But Gloria continued to insist that gunning for Templar was a waste of time and resources; Dick Westergard was still the one to beat.

The worst part, though, was the feeling that she had absolutely no control over what was happening. It reminded her of her first time on a sled. Growing up in southern California, she hadn't had any experience with snow. The first heavy snowfall after she came to Rose Hill thrilled her. When a classmate invited her to come sledding in the park, she went without a second thought. When she found herself sliding ever faster down a steep hill however, panic seized her. Trees lined either side of the slope, and at the bottom was a stone wall and a busy street. Halfway down, she realized that her fate was entirely out of her hands. All she could do was close her eyes, grip the handholds, and wait for the end, whatever it might be.

As she sat in her room trying to make notes for her presentation at the candidates' forum the next day, she found herself longing for the campaign to end. She was worn out, both physically and emotionally. She no longer knew whether she was likely to win, and she realized with a small shock that she no longer cared very much, either. She wanted to be able to feel that she had run a good race, but it didn't really matter whether she or Dick was next year's vice-president. What mattered much more was trying to dispel the antagonism that had seized the school. No doubt Lars had seen B.E.S.T. at work, and knew she was associated with it. Her victory would mean nothing in his eyes compared to the undemocratic campaign B.E.S.T. had run.

On an impulse, she picked up the telephone and called information for Dick's home number. If she could only talk to him, maybe they could find ways to cool down the situation. As she was about to dial, however, she recalled his face as he snubbed her in the hall on Friday. He hadn't looked like someone who would welcome a call from her. He might even hang up when he found out who it was. She wasn't sure she could stand one more humiliation, especially from someone she wanted to like her. Once again she reflected, her brilliant plan for revenge had not only backfired, it had hurt her more than anyone else.

In the meantime, she had to prepare for the forum. She gnawed on the cap of her pen as she considered her presentation. Gloria had wanted to write a speech for her that directly attacked Dick's platform and the strong-arm tactics of his supporters, but Laurie had refused. There had been too much of that kind of campaigning already. All she wanted to do was say what she thought was wrong with student government and how she would change it if elected.

She had written down a list of essential points to remember in her notebook. When she looked for it in her bookbag, however, it wasn't there. She remembered putting it in her locker, along with a bunch of other things before gym, but she couldn't recall if she had retrieved it later. The incidents at lunch and afterward had driven everything else from her mind.

Frowning, she tried to reconstruct the list. But when she finished she was sure that there were important points left out. She glanced at her watch. Not quite four-thirty; the building would be open for another hour or so. It would be faster to zip over and get her notebook, than to try to make up the list again. In any case, she was tired of sitting in an empty house; if she went somewhere, it might create the illusion of accomplishing something.

There were still three or four cars in the parking lot. She pulled up near the entrance and walked toward her locker. The only sound in the empty corridor was the swish of her soft-soled suede boots on the hard floor. It gave her a creepy feeling. She had occasionally had to go somewhere during a class period when the halls were just as empty as this, but there was always a murmur of voices from the rooms. This total silence was like something from a high school horror movie.

Laurie was beginning to wish she had stayed home when, from around the corner ahead, she heard the welcome sound of a boy and girl talking and laughing. The creepy feeling evaporated at once. She smiled to herself. It was so easy to imagine the worst when you were all alone.

Maybe that was the real cause of the hostility in the campaign for vice-president, Laurie thought. She and Dick might both simply be imagining that the other campaign was fighting dirty, then responding in kind to the products of their imaginations. Perhaps the whole conflict was between two sets of phantoms! But then she reminded herself that the ripped-down posters and stolen newspapers were not imaginary. Someone was responsible for those incidents.

At that moment she turned the corner, and found herself face to face with her campaign manager. Gloria had her arms around a boy who seemed to be chuckling over something she had just said. Funny, Laurie thought, Gloria never mentioned a boyfriend. The boy must have felt her stiffen when she saw Laurie, because he turned to look over his shoulder.

It was Farley Templar.

Laurie stood quite still, frowning in concentration, trying to comprehend. Then, as if a dam had broken, the truth rushed in and overwhelmed her. Gloria had planted herself in Laurie's campaign; she had been working for her boyfriend Farley all along. The two of them had started the fire and deliberately fanned the flames, to bog down Laurie and Dick in a fight with each other, and allow Farley to present himself as the reasonable alternative. No wonder Gloria had insisted she ignore Farley and concentrate on Dick.

Farley was trying to put on an innocent look, but it kept slipping, and revealing the fright underneath. He, at least, understood what a gamble he had taken and knew that he had almost certainly lost. Gloria, however, was smirking as if she had done something remarkably clever. Laurie could almost imagine her asking her to congratulate her for coming so close to pulling it off.

All the things she might do, from attacking Gloria bodily to telephoning the principal, flashed through Laurie's mind, but none of them came close to fitting the situation. She finally turned on her heel and walked away without a word.

The walk back to the car and the drive home happened as if she had been programmed. During the whole trip, the week's incidents played in her mind. Once home, she wandered aimlessly around the downstairs for a while, then climbed the stairs to her room. The crumpled leaflet for Templar was still in the middle of the floor. She stepped around it as gingerly, as if it were a snake, and lay down on the bed.

Farley and Gloria were probably still back at school laughing at her at that very moment. How her gullibility must have amazed them! She had made it so easy. She had taken Gloria completely at face value and put her in charge of her entire campaign. She had even been happy to think that she had found a good friend, as well as a co-worker.

Her face burned as she realized how completely she had been manipulated. Gloria had never actually asked to be campaign manager. Instead, she had maneuvered Laurie into offering her the job. It had been like that every step of the way. Whenever she thought she was making her own decisions, Gloria had been subtly forcing her toward the decisions *she* wanted.

What Laurie hated most was the way they had abused her trust. She had never had much sympathy for people whose greed and vanity made them natural targets for con men. In a way, it was their own faults that opened them to being victimized. As the saying went, they had no one but themselves to blame.

Gloria had flattered Laurie continually from the moment they met. That had been part of the reason Laurie accepted her so readily. She had turned a blind eye to what Gloria was doing in her name. She had practically asked to be fooled, even *deserved* to be fooled. Knowing that made her feel no better about having been taken in. If anything, it made her feel worse by piling guilt on top of mistreatment.

Lying on her bed brooding wasn't doing her any good. It was pulling her deeper into a bog of self-pity. What she really needed was to talk to someone about this, someone she could trust to listen sympathetically, and to respond honestly. She stood up and went to the telephone, then stopped with her hand on the receiver. She had no one to call.

Ridiculous! She knew loads of people. She began to thumb through her address book. A great many names and numbers were there, but that didn't help. Most of them were people she would invite to a big party, not people she would pour out her soul to. As she continued to look, she began to realize that there was not one person there that she was genuinely close to. Since coming to Rose Hill over a year ago, she had done everything she could to make herself popular. But in all that time she had not made a single friend.

What was wrong with her? Was it something she lacked, some ability that other people had naturally, but that had been left out of her makeup? The image of Gloria as she had last seen her came into her mind: that look of smug superiority, of satisfaction at her own cleverness. She knew that look very well, because she had felt it in the deepest layers of her own face. Beneath the skin, Gloria and she were twins.

She suddenly remembered Lisa Chang, the champion skater, and the way she had manipulated her into running for homecoming princess against Chris Austin. She still felt that a potential Olympic athlete like Lisa deserved to be honored by her school, and that Chris had won more on the strength of whom she knew than what she had done, but that no longer mattered. What did matter was that she had never been honest with Lisa, never told her frankly that she was as much interested in seeing Chris lose as in seeing Lisa win. She had tried to use Lisa. She had even felt smug about the cleverness of her scheme. When Lisa eventually found out, of course, she dropped out of the contest and refused to speak to Laurie again. So maybe the scheme hadn't been so clever after all. Chris had won the homecoming title, and Laurie had lost a possible friend.

Laurie couldn't remember why she cared so much about being clever, anyway. It obviously was not the path to popularity. People laughed at her snide remarks and put-downs, but they didn't like her better for them. No wonder people edged away from her; they knew that they might be the next target! No reasonable person would

160

trust someone who might at any moment turn his confidence into the raw material for a joke.

The reason she had no friends was obvious: She didn't know how to be a friend. She had never felt the need or taken the trouble to find out.

Laurie could change, she was sure of it. And she was *going* to change. Now that she saw what she had been doing wrong, she had a chance to find out how to do it right. She was going to seize that chance and become a new person, a much better person — a person worthy of having friends and enjoying their trust.

She felt lifted up by her commitment to change. But she also felt a great need to share it with someone who would appreciate what it meant. A warm, open face presented itself to her. She grabbed a jacket, and ran down the stairs. She knew if she stopped to think, she would lose her nerve. The Mustang's top was still down from the afternoon, but she flicked on the heater and left it like that.

The drive to the Westergard house took no more than five minutes, but that was enough time for Laurie to have second thoughts. His parents had only met her once, for a few minutes. Even if they remembered her, he had probably told them all about what had been going on at school, so they weren't going to be very glad to see her.

And Dick didn't know what she knew, so there was no reason to think he'd be happy to see her. The last time they had come face to face, he had been unbending in the face of her arguments. A lot had happened since then, but none of it was likely to make him any friendlier toward her. As far as he knew, she was responsible for running a campaign against him that was one of the dirtiest anyone at Kennedy High School could remember. As far as he knew, she was still right in the middle of it. If he saw her on his doorstep, he would probably suspect that it was some kind of trap, and would have every right to that suspicion.

As she sat in her car, across the dark street from his home, she began to imagine the scene behind the lighted windows. Dick was sitting at the dinner table doing his homework, and his little sisters were sprawled on the floor doing theirs. His mother was reading a book, and his father was examining a chess problem. Or perhaps the whole family was sitting together, laughing over some comedy on TV.

As she thought of them, so close, and of the empty house she had to go back to, she began to cry. At first only a few tears trickled silently down her cheeks, but soon she was lost in desolate sobs. There was so much that she had missed and could never have. If one of Dick's sisters was lonely or hurt, she would never be left to cry alone. But Laurie had no one to comfort her, no one to assure her that this pain would pass, that life still held out promise.

"Do you want me to fix that top again?" a voice said. "It looks like it's turning wet."

"Dick!" she said, laughing through her sobs. "What are you doing here?"

He vaulted over the side of the car, into the passenger seat. "I'm checking out a report of a suspicious stranger parked on our block. Hi, stranger."

"Hi," she said in a whisper. She swallowed, collected her courage, and began, "Dick, I want to tell you — "

"Laurie, I've been wanting — "

They both stopped in confusion. Then, before she could speak, he rushed into the silence. "I have to apologize for the other day. It's no excuse, but, well, Anne and Melissa had spent a whole evening drawing an election poster for me. It was beautiful. Just before I saw you that day, I'd found it torn to bits. I was so mad I didn't know what to do. It wasn't fair to blame you, I know, but I jumped to the easiest conclusion. I've felt rotten about it ever since. Will you forgive me?"

"Of course," she said breathlessly. "But there's something you should know. In a way, I *was* responsible." She told him what she had discovered about Gloria and Farley Templar, and what she thought it meant. Before he could get done exclaiming over their plot, she rushed into an analysis of her own character, with special emphasis on its weaknesses and failings. She even told him about Lisa Chang and the election for homecoming princess. The more she said, the more doleful her voice became. Finally she sighed, and said, "I don't supposed you'll have any more to do with someone that awful. I'd better go home and stop bothering you."

She leaned forward to turn the ignition key, but there was something in her way. A strong arm

163

came around her shoulders, and gentle fingers clasped her chin to turn her face toward him. Then his lips were on hers once more, warm and soft, yet undeniable. The tensions and doubts, and feelings of worthlessness crept away, no match for her sure knowledge that he cared for her. When he released her, she gasped for breath. Then she twined her fingers in his hair and pulled him down to her again.

After another timeless moment, he began to nuzzle her neck while she held onto his. Each deep breath brought her the scent of his hair, and she was unwilling to let go. "I should go," he finally murmured. "They probably think I've been abducted by the suspicious stranger."

"You have," she whispered. "Come home with me now."

"I can't, Laurie. I wish I could. I have to work on my presentation for the forum tomorrow. Which reminds me: What are we going to do Templar and his double-agent girl friend?"

"*I'll* take care of them," she said grimly. "I won't tell you what I'm planning, but you'll know when I've done it. And so will they!"

Chapter
16

The audience was filling quickly. Sasha edged through a clump of freshman boys who were tossing a wad of paper back and forth, and reclaimed her seat in the fourth row. For the fifth time she checked the battery level of her borrowed microcassette recorder. She had complete faith in her ability to take notes the old-fashioned way with a pencil and pad. But given the amount of controversy the election had aroused, she wanted to have a backup in case someone accused her of misquoting.

Not that her story about today's forum was going to make the least bit of difference. The next issue of the paper wasn't due out until after the election — too late to affect anything, and too early to report the results. She flipped to the back of her notepad, and jotted a reminder to suggest to student government that future elections take place on a Monday, so that the votes could be released in that week's *The Red and the Gold.*

Politically speaking, the paper was going to be in very good shape next year, whatever happened tomorrow. Chris was a good friend who understood the importance of the press, and appreciated the paper's endorsement of her. As SG president she would listen sympathetically to the problems of running a school newspaper and do what she could to help. If John managed to win the race instead, it still would not be a disaster. He didn't like the endorsement of Chris, but he had somehow managed to get a copy of the vandalized issue and had read his interview. He had the sense to see that it was rather favorable toward him. In fact, he even wondered aloud if Chris's supporters might have dumped the paper for that reason.

That was absurd, of course, but Sasha still could not figure out who might have done it and why. Brad had announced that student council was offering a reward for information about the perpetrators, but no one had come forward. Every time she thought about somebody ruining an entire edition of her newspaper, she clenched her fists so tightly that her nails left marks. As Wes had said on Sunday, in the midst of consoling her, it was enough to make her forget she was a pacifist.

The candidates were filing onto the stage. Most of them looked as if their hands were recent purchases that they hadn't yet found a place for. After the usual confusion of finding seats, they all sat down and Brad came forward to the rostrum.

"Is this thing on?" his voice boomed. "Oh,

okay." He cleared his throat thunderously. "On behalf of Kennedy High School Student Government, I'd like to welcome you to the very first of what we hope will be an annual series of forums presenting the candidates for school office. Let me explain how we're going to do this. First we'll hear from those running for student council — first freshmen, then sophomores and juniors."

"What about seniors, Brad?" someone called.

"We've got other things on our minds," he quipped, "like getting into college. And this afternoon will go a lot smoother if we keep down comments from the floor. After the student council candidates, we'll hear those who are running for school offices — secretary, treasurer, vice-president, and president, in that order. For each office, the different candidates have tossed a coin to decide the order in which they will speak.

"If that's clear, I'd like to introduce our first candidate for freshman representative, Binky Tiernan."

A pale girl with a dark ponytail bobbed up. She explained that she wanted to be on student council and hoped everyone would vote for her. Then she sat down. Brad, who had expected a longer speech, was taken by surprise and had to fumble for his list of speakers.

Sasha did not exactly tune out, but she stopped listening intently. She often used this technique at meetings. The stream of words flowed past her unheeded. But she was sure she could count on noticing if anything unusual or newsworthy was said, most of the time nothing was.

The student council candidates seemed as eager

as the audience to get to the two main events of the day, the contestants for vice-president and president. Most of them were almost as brief as the first girl. One or two who seemed inclined to speak longer had to face an outbreak of coughs, throat clearings, and shuffling, and soon gave up. To make matters simpler, the candidate for secretary was unopposed, and there was only one serious candidate for treasurer — a sophomore who had spent this year working as assistant treasurer.

Finally Brad said, "There are three candidates for vice-president: Farley Templar, Laurie Bennington, and Richard Westergard. They will give their presentations in that order. Farley Templar."

Sasha studied him curiously as he took the podium. He was wearing a dark blue, three-piece suit and striped tie. He had obviously had an expensive barber deal with his dark, glossy hair very recently. She was ready to bet that if she got close to him, she would catch a whiff of some designer cologne. Young man on the move, she thought, giving the words a sardonic twist, as if to ask where he was on the move to.

"My fellow students," he began, "personality conflicts and petty squabbles have no place in student government. What we need is an efficient, businesslike, and above all, a dignified administration."

Sasha sat up straighter and opened her eyes wide. Good grief, the guy was quoting from his own leaflets! She listened closely and checked off the sentences as they went by. As near as she could tell, only one — something obscure about zero-based budgeting — was not word for word from the literature his supporters had been passing out for the last few days. She gave an amused snort; at least he was saving her the trouble of taking notes!

She was surprised by the amount of applause when he finished. She guessed that a lot of kids had been turned off by the bitter arguing the campaign had set off, and took Templar on his own terms as a businesslike and dignified alternative. She jotted a couple of quick notes, then looked up as Brad introduced Laurie.

The first surprise was the way Laurie looked. Her dark hair was simply and attractively arranged, and whatever makeup she had on was doing its job without being apparent. Her white dress, of some crinkly linen material, did have a wide neck that showed off her shoulders; but its length, to just above the knee, was almost conservative. The only touch of her usual flamboyance was a bright silk sash tied loosely at the waist.

"When I decided to run for vice-president," she began, "I asked myself what I thought was important in student government." Her tone was the second surprise for Sasha. Far from being harsh or brittle, it was soft, tentative, almost intimate. "My first thought was that openness, accessibility, came first. We should all be able to get involved, and *want* to get involved, in what our representatives are doing. I still think that is terribly important. But in the past few days, I have learned that another quality is even more essential. That quality is trust."

She paused to scan the audience, seeming to stop and stare at one particular person. Sasha glanced around, but couldn't tell who it was.

"I know most of you have been surprised and disturbed by the hostility this election has stirred up," Laurie continued. "So was I. I couldn't understand it. My supporters were accused of all sorts of underhanded tactics — "

"They were guilty!" someone called out. Brad started up out of his chair, then sat down again as Laurie held up a hand.

" — and so were those who favored my chief opponent, Dick Westergard."

From the back of the room, a few people began to chant, "Westergard! Westergard!" Others chanted, "B-E-S-T! B-E-S-T!" Brad stood up and exchanged a glance with Laurie, who looked paler now. But the mass of the audience turned to glare at the chanters and silence them, and soon the room was quiet again.

Laurie resumed in a stronger voice. "Yesterday I found out that someone I had trusted, someone I had looked on as a friend as well as a supporter, was secretly working for an opponent of mine. My campaign manager, Gloria MacMillan, is actually a very close friend of Farley Templar, who just asked you to elect him vice-president."

In the hubbub this statement provoked, someone was screaming, "That's a lie!" Gloria was on her feet, shaking her fist at the stage. Sasha realized that it was she, whom Laurie had been staring at.

"It's the truth!" Laurie shouted. "And I believe that the two of them have been behind all the ugly incidents that have so disgusted all of us. They planned the whole thing, to create so much ill feeling between the other candidates that you turned to Farley Templar as a sensible alternative. But it didn't work. It won't work. You won't stand for that kind of underhandedness in people who ask for your trust."

"I'm not going to listen to this garbage!" Templar jumped up and stalked off the stage. There was a stir in the hall as Gloria, and three or four others, walked out ostentatiously.

Laurie waited until they were gone, then said, "I told you their plot won't work. But there's one way that it might still work. If some of you vote for me and some of you vote for my honorable opponent Dick Westergard, that divided vote just might permit my *dis*honorable opponent, Farley Templar, to win. I can't allow that to happen, so I am withdrawing from the race. Thanks to all of you who supported me, and I urge you as strongly as I can, to give your wholehearted support, as I do, to our next vice-president, Dick Westergard!"

As the audience exploded in cheers, she walked over, took Dick's hand, and pulled him to the rostrum. Her cheeks were damp, Sasha noted, but she was wearing a wide smile. Dick looked bewildered; in fact, he seemed to be conducting a whispered argument with Laurie. Finally, he turned to the audience and held up his hands for silence.

"I don't know what to say," he began. The

audience chuckled sympathetically. "By the time Laurie finished speaking, I was ready to vote for her myself. If I could convince her to withdraw her withdrawal — does that make sense? — I would."

"No way!" Laurie called from the sidelines.

He shrugged. "You all heard her. And I don't have to tell you how determined she is. So the choice comes down to me or Farley Templar. We don't have all the facts about Laurie's accusations, so I'm not going to say anything more about them." After scattered applause and a brief pause, Dick read his prepared speech. Then he gave an abrupt, almost awkward, nod and left the rostrum. Once again the audience exploded. Sasha was surprised by the enthusiasm. She thought he had spoken well and made some important points, but it hadn't seemed like a speech that would bring an audience to its feet. Yet it, or the drama of Laurie's withdrawal, or the combined impact of the two, had done just that.

Brad waited patiently by the microphone until the applause died down. "Our next speaker, one of two candidates for president of the Kennedy High School student body, is John Marquette."

As the chant of "B-E-S-T!" started again, John walked to the podium. He had dressed for the occasion in black jeans and a black T-shirt with a B.E.S.T. armband on his left arm. As he stood waiting for the chanters to be quiet, his eyes seemed to recede into his head and his jaw to protrude. Finally he raised both arms in a gesture of command, and the chanters shut up.

172

"I listened to what Westergard just said," he began, "and you can take it from me, it was a lot of hot air. What you want is a student government that'll take care of you, right? But that takes strong leadership. Why doesn't student council get anything down now? Because they're too busy debating, and sitting around mouthing off, that's why. Well, when I'm president, I'll see to it that that changes, or else."

Some people laughed. He stared at them, then held up a piece of paper. "This is a list of the things I'm going to do as president. I won't go over it now, but take my word, there's something there for just about everybody. If you haven't seen it yet, ask anybody with a B.E.S.T. armband to give you a copy. And *save it* — because what I say I'm going to do, I'm *going* to do. If student council doesn't like it, they can go soak their heads. Hey, if they hassle me too much, maybe I'll soak their heads for them, huh, huh!"

Sasha was scribbling madly, trying to get John's entire speech verbatim. She fervently hoped the recorder was getting it, too; she wanted to play it back for her mom and dad.

"Just one more thing," he continued. "Some of you may be wondering why you should vote for me, and not my opponent. After all, she's a lot better looking, huh, huh!" That drew a few scattered boos and hisses. John scowled. "We'll deal with you later. As I was saying, why vote for me? Because you have to have strong leaders to take care of you, that's why. Chris Austin is a nice girl, but she ought to stick to running the Honor Society, and leave the real work to those of us

173

who have what it takes to do it. That's all."

As he walked back to his seat, the boos were louder and more widespread. But it seemed to Sasha that the cheers were louder, too. How was Chris going to deal with this?

Chris stepped up to the microphone wearing a classic-print shirtwaist that perfectly complemented her all-American good looks. Sasha made a bet with herself that the dress had been specially designed by Henry Braverman. The applause that greeted her was strong, but not fervent. When it died, she showed the audience a sheaf of typewritten pages.

"This is the speech I came here to give," she said in a clear voice. "I put in a lot of work on it, believe me. I wanted it to be the most perfect speech I knew how to give." She grasped the manuscript in both hands, tore it in two, and let the pieces flutter to the floor. Over the gasps from the audience, she continued. "Some amazing things have happened here this afternoon, and they've made me do a lot of thinking while I've been sitting up here waiting for my turn. I want to share some of those thoughts with you."

She leaned her elbow on the podium and spoke almost chattily into the microphone. "I find myself agreeing with what Laurie said, that the most important quality those who want to hold public office need is trust. But trust is a two-way proposition. I ask you to trust me to look after your interests, but I have to trust that you are mature and sensible enough to know your own interests far better than I ever can. What we owe each other is the benefit of the doubt whenever we disagree . . . and I'm sure we will disagree many times. It's a lot like friendship; when our friends do things we don't understand or maybe don't like, we owe it to them to think the best of it, not the worst. That's one of the important lessons this campaign has taught me.

"Another is that we all make mistakes. Take that perfect speech of mine." She pointed to the scraps on the stage. "In it, I urged you to elect Farley Templar as my vice-president because both Laurie Bennington and Richard Westergard had used tactics that disgraced them. As some of you know — say, anyone who was within fifty miles of the quad last Friday — I have already made some similar statements out loud."

That drew a knowing laugh, but Chris's face was totally serious as she said, "I was wrong, utterly, and completely wrong, and I apologize to Laurie. I drew the conclusions that I meant to draw, but that is no excuse. The fact is, I was ready, even willing, to think the worst. I was trying to be inhumanly perfect, and I expected that same inhuman perfection from those around me. When they failed, as of course they had to, I blamed them, rather than see that I was at fault for expecting too much. They know who they are, and they, too, deserve an apology."

She straightened up. "By now some of you may be wondering why you should vote for someone who keeps making mistakes and apologizing for them. You've heard that what you need is a strong leader who will look after you. If that's what you want, somebody to hold your hand and tell you what to do, I'm not it. If I'm elected, I expect you to be my partners, not my charges. And if being strong means not recognizing or admitting mistakes, I'd say no thanks. But I don't accept that meaning. To me, strength means the ability to listen to criticism, to see where you've gone off the track, and to own up to your mistakes. I believe I am developing that kind of strength, and if I am elected I mean to use it. Thank you."

She was halfway off the stage before the audience realized that she had finished. In an instant they were on their feet, clapping and cheering. Sasha was on her feet, too, though she squared that with her journalistic neutrality by not shouting. Her dearest wish at that moment was for a close-up color photo of John Marquette's glowering face. She would hang it on her wall, and look at it any time she started to wonder if there was any justice in the world.

As the other candidates left the stage, Laurie sat in her chair waiting for the crowd to clear. She didn't want anyone to see her with smudged mascara under her eyes. In the back of the auditorium, she saw Lars looking her way, and realized that she hadn't even thought to look for him as she made her speech. The whole idea that she had run for office just to spite him seemed like a bad dream from which she had long ago awakened. She was through with plots and schemes. Nothing good had come of any of the clever plans she had devised over the course of the past year.

She felt a hand on her shoulder and looked up to see Chris Austin beside her. Chris wordlessly extended her right hand, and Laurie solemnly shook it. Then the moment grew awkward, and Chris smiled and walked on. Laurie was glad to have earned the respect of someone she was beginning to admire more and more.

As she rose to go, another hand reached out for her, gently grasping her arm. "I still think I could have beat you," Dick teased, as he pulled her toward him.

"Maybe so," she replied. "But now we'll never know."

"Do you think it's a little early for a private victory celebration?" Dick asked.

"I don't think so," Laurie replied. "Pizza with the girls, maybe?"

"That's not exactly what I had in mind." Dick smiled as he moved his hand from Laurie's arm to her waist, and pulled her toward him. As Laurie turned to hold him, she looked across the stage to the auditorium door.

There stood a fuming Gloria, next to Farley Templar, who had lost his young-man-on-the-move composure. "I don't believe it!" Laurie heard Gloria exclaim. "She double-crossed us!"

Laurie couldn't resist waving at her campaign manager before she bent to take in the warmth that was becoming so comfortable and familiar to her. From the back of the auditorium came gasps of surprise, and then friendly applause. For a moment, she wondered if Lars was among the stragglers. But her thoughts were erased by the softness of Dick's lips against hers, and she couldn't be bothered to look.

Chapter **17**

Phoebe looked around the lunch table, counting heads. The whole bunch was there. At the far end was Chris, doing her best not to look nervous. A smiling, confident Ted was on one side of her, and Kim was on the other. Next to Ted was Brenda, and Brad, of course, was next to her, holding her hand and talking in a low tone. Then came Henry and Janie, who were deep in a conversation about decorations for the senior prom.

From his seat next to Kim, Woody looked down the table, caught Phoebe's glance, and winked. She was glad that they had sorted out their problems. And she was glad that Chris and Ted were back to their normal relationship. She wasn't one bit jealous of them, but she couldn't help constantly comparing their happiness with her own separation from the boy she loved.

Sasha, across the table, was looking glum.

"Hey," Phoebe said. "Cheer up, it'll soon be over, whatever it is."

Sasha made a face. "I'm sorry, Pheeb," she said. "I'm just so furious that I have to sit here in the lunchroom, waiting to hear the most important news at Kennedy this year. And from Peter Lacey of all people! It's humiliating! Peter wouldn't know a news story if it bit him on the bottom!"

Phoebe laughed. "Even he knows this one is news. Speaking of news, did you notice who's sitting four tables behind me?"

Sasha glanced past her. Laurie Bennington and Dick Westergard were sitting next to each other with their chairs pulled very close together. "Hmph," Sasha said. "One of these days, Phoebe, I'll explain to you the difference between news and gossip."

"Shhh!" Brenda had her finger to her lips and was pointing to the ceiling speaker with the other hand.

As the lunchroom hum faded, Phoebe heard Peter saying, ". . . to hear the results of Wednesday's election. To take it from the top, then: in the race for president, the vote was: Christine Austin, six hundred forty-four, and John Marquette, three hundred eighteen."

"Yippee!" Ted sprang to his feet, grabbed Chris by the waist, and tossed her into the air. On the way down, he caught her and gave her an enthusiastic kiss. "Sweetheart," he said loudly, "you — "

"*Shhhhh!*"

". . . race for vice-president, here is the tally.

179

Farley Templar, two hundred thirty-three votes; Richard Westergard, six hundred twenty-seven votes; and one hundred two write-in votes for Laurie Bennington."

Phoebe looked around. Dick's friends were cheering and clapping him on the back. Laurie was standing to one side with a smile on her face that seemed to flicker. Then Dick reached an arm out for her, and the smile returned to full voltage.

"Pheeb?" Chris's voice said in her ear. "Do you really and truly forgive me?"

"You idiot," Phoebe cried. "Of course I do!" She gave her friend a warm hug. "And congratulations," she added. "You deserved to win if anyone ever did."

Then a crowd of well-wishers surrounded Chris, and Phoebe lost sight of her.

Now that the suspense of the election was over, she felt a little empty. She no longer had something to keep her mind off her own problems. When Griffin had called, two nights before, she hadn't known what to say. He had been bubbling over with enthusiasm about the play, his part, and his fellow actors — even the director, who he described as being tough as nails and sharp as a tack. When he asked directly if she was coming, she had stalled. She could still hear the disappointment in his voice. She had never disobeyed her parents on anything really important, and she didn't want to now. But she and Griffin were in love, and he needed her.

"Hey, Pheeb-a-re-bop, a-bop-bam-boom! I need to talk to you."

She gave Woody a fond smile. "Talk. I'm listening."

"Listen, I was talking to my mom last night."

"Lots of talking and listening going on," she observed.

"Stop talking and listen! My mom has to go to New York on business. A friend of hers is lending her her loft in Soho."

"Yes?" Phoebe said hopefully.

"What would your mom and dad say if my mom's trip happened to be on the same weekend as Griffin's workshop, and she happened to invite you to come along?"

It took a moment to sink in. "Woody!" she gasped. "Could she? Would she? Really?"

"Would she, could she . . . sounds like a nursery rhyme."

She grabbed his arm and squeezed it. "Please, be serious! Do you mean it?"

He nodded. "Mom will give your folks a call tonight."

"That's *fabulous*!" She threw her arms around him and gave him a big kiss on the cheek. He turned bright red. "Oh, I can't wait!"

In the control room of WKND, Peter came to the end of the list of student council candidates and their vote totals. "And that's the story about the vote-ee-oh-dohs, Cardinals. Now back to the music. Here's a hot new cassette by a backroom bar band from Augusta, Georgia. They call themselves the Longneck Bottle Band, after their favorite brew. But after you listen, maybe you'll

181

think they should change that to Redneck! Anyway, you can say you heard it here first, even if you never hear it anywhere else!"

He faded the mike and cranked up the volume on the cassette. A torrent of basic two-chord rock 'n' roll poured from the studio monitor and he sat back to relax for three minutes, seventeen seconds. He put one hand to his shirt pocket, but did not pull out Lisa's letter. He had read it over so many times that he practically knew it by heart.

She wrote all about practice and workouts, and more practice. She wrote about the nationally-ranked track stars, swimmers, and gymnasts she had met, and practiced with and studied with. She wrote about the former Olympians who came to coach, and offer clinics, and advice. Then she said she missed him, and all her friends, and talking about old times. *Love,* Lisa.

Was that what he had become, then? One of her old friends? They had fallen totally in love, but before they had any time together, Lisa had been offered the scholarship to the training program. A few days later she was gone. He thought of her, even dreamed of her, but he wasn't sure he even knew her anymore. It had to change a person to be living among the best athletes of a generation. She soon might have nothing to say to some ordinary guy whose only distinction was that he used to love her.

The cassette roared to an end. With a practiced twist he flicked up the mike level and said enthusiastically, "Hey, hey, a hit? Or a miss? It's up to you. And next, one from The Boss."

182

Coming Soon...
Couples #8
Making Promises

Peter turned around so his back was to the control panel. He leaned back against the counter, stretching out his sweat suit-clad legs. He looked up at Monica and grinned. She found his lopsided smile endearing.

"I know we haven't had time to talk much since you've started working here," Peter said. "I just wanted to let you know I'm grateful for your help."

"Oh, it's nothing," Monica said.

"Don't be modest. Since you've been here I haven't made any screw-ups over the air. That means an awful lot to me."

Monica was sure her face was blushing as red as a stoplight. She lowered her head so Peter wouldn't notice, and began to back out of the room.

But he wasn't through. "Wait a second, Monica. I sort of have a favor to ask. I know Henry left the library a real mess, and I was wondering if you wouldn't mind staying after school on Monday to help me sort it out. I'm expecting more records in over the weekend, too, so we'll really have our work cut out for us."

"I wouldn't mind coming in and helping." Monica surprised herself with that offer.

"Great." Peter smiled and walked toward her. "You know, Monica, I think you may be the best thing that ever happened to this radio station."

We hope you enjoyed reading this book. All the titles currently available in the Couples series are listed on Page Two. They are all available at your local bookshop or newsagent, though should you find any difficulty in obtaining the books you would like, you can order direct from the publisher, at the address below. Also, if you would like to know more about the series, or would simply like to tell us what you think of the series, write to:

Kim Prior,
Couples,
Transworld Publishers Limited,
61–63 Uxbridge Road,
Ealing, London W5 5SA.

To order books, please list the title(s) you would like, and send together with your name and address, and a cheque or postal order made payable to TRANSWORLD PUBLISHERS LIMITED. Please allow cost of book(s) plus 20p for the first book and 10p for each additional book for postage and packing. Please note that payment must be made in UK currency; Irish currency is not acceptable.

(The above applies to readers in the UK and Ireland only.)

If you live in Australia or New Zealand, and would like more information about the series, please write to:

Sally Porter,
Couples,
Corgi & Bantam Books,
26 Harley Crescent,
Condell Park,
N.S.W. 2200,
Australia.

Kiri Martin,
Couples,
c/o Corgi & Bantam Books New Zealand,
Cnr. Moselle and Waipareira Avenues,
Henderson,
Auckland,
New Zealand.

WINNERS

by Suzanne Rand

A great new mini-series . . .

Being seventeen can be great fun – as Stacy Harcourt, Gina
Damone and Tess Belding discover as they enter their exciting
senior year at Midvale High School. Apart from years of
friendship, the popular trio share their main interests in common –
an obsession with cheerleading in the elite school squad, and
boys! For all three girls, the intricate gymnastic jumps and
routines of their favourite hobby are the best things in their lives –
but the gorgeous footballers they are supporting are definitely
the icing on the cake! Picked to lead the cheering, the girls know
they have one of the school's highest honours and a big
responsibility to be the best that they can be in every way.

Each book highlights the story of one of the girls.

1. **THE GIRL MOST LIKELY**
2. **ALL AMERICAN GIRL**
3. **CAREER GIRL**

WINNERS – available wherever Bantam paperbacks are sold!